DOUBLE CHECK

For Rosemary Bromley

KINGFISHER

An imprint of Kingfisher Publications Plc
New Penderel House, 283-288 High Holborn
London WC1V 7HZ
www.kingfisherpub.com

This edition published by Kingfisher 2007
First published by Kingfisher 2006
2 4 6 8 10 9 7 5 3 1

A CIP catalogue record for this book
is available from the British Library.

ISBN 978 0 7534 1492 7

Printed in India
1TR/0307/THOM/(THOM)/80TORA/C

TRACES

DOUBLE CHECK

MALCOLM ROSE

KINGFISHER

ABOUT THE AUTHOR

Malcolm Rose, a former Senior Lecturer in Chemistry, is a well-known children's thriller writer of some 25 novels including five *Traces* titles. Malcolm has won the Angus Book Award and the Lancashire Book of the Year Award. His books regularly feature in the Book Trust 100 best books for children list. In the USA, *Traces: Framed!* was selected as a Best International Book by the International Reading Association. Malcolm lives in Sheffield.

Chapter One

A shiver enveloped the official executioner's body when he stepped into the empty Death Cell. He always reacted badly to the dreadful atmosphere as he entered the cold chamber in Block J of Cambridge Prison. Greg Roper didn't let the unpleasant prickling put him off, though. To distract himself, he imagined how he'd been chosen as executioner. Of all the prison guards, he had the name that sounded most like the Grim Reaper. Really, being called Greg Roper had nothing to do with his job, but the thought brought an ironic smile to his lips. When he was preparing the Death Cell, he needed an excuse to smile.

There were no windows and only two pieces of furniture in the small room: a bed that could be tilted from almost upright to horizontal and a wooden cabinet on wheels. First, Greg opened the cabinet and checked that the chemicals were all present and correct. Sodium pentothal would put the prisoner to sleep. Pancuronium bromide would paralyse his lungs and diaphragm, then potassium chloride would stop his heart. The whole process of delivering the death sentence was designed to take between fifteen and twenty minutes. Greg was proud of his record: thirteen and a half minutes from strapping of the inmate onto the bed to the ending of life. After all, he didn't want to prolong the suffering, even of a murderer.

He checked that there was enough saline solution to wash the tubes that would deliver the fatal sequence of chemicals. He measured the tubes to make sure that they were long enough and then he inspected both intravenous needles. One would be placed in the criminal's arm and the other was a spare in case something went wrong. Not that the procedure had ever gone wrong in Greg's hands.

Satisfied, he turned his attention to the bed and said to the computer, "Upright position, please." Greg whispered really. He always whispered in the Death Cell. With its belts and fastenings dangling grimly, the bed tipped slowly until it was almost vertical. It came to a halt without a hint of shuddering. Everything had to be perfect. Perfectly smooth was how Greg liked it. That's why he practised, checked and double-checked well before an execution. "Project a life-size hologram of Everton Kohter onto it, please."

The image didn't look totally like the real thing. It was a mere ghost of a man. Or boy in this case. In nineteen days, Everton would become the smallest, youngest person that Greg had ever strapped onto the bed. He knelt down and made sure that the lower ties were correctly adjusted to attach to the prisoner's ankles. He didn't want to have to fiddle with the buckles while the poor boy waited to die. The long belts that would encircle his waist and chest seemed fine. At the top of the bed, the forehead loop needed to be five millimetres shorter to stop Everton jerking his head. Greg wanted it tight so that the prisoner could not possibly damage himself if he struggled.

Finally, Greg ensured that the arm restraints were functioning properly and set for Everton's measurements. Once the intravenous needle was in place under his skin, it was vital that the prisoner could not free an arm from the strap and thrash around. That way, he could dislodge the delivery tube.

Content, Greg said in a hushed voice, "That's all. End program."

The virtual version of Everton Kohter disappeared at once. When the real thing had been put to sleep and the prison doctor had pronounced bleakly, "Life extinct," Greg would call in two of his colleagues to take the body away. And hopefully he would be able to congratulate himself on an efficient job well done.

It was no use telling The Authorities that he was alone in his hotel room. Luke knew that Jade would keep very quiet, he was sure he could lie confidently and persuasively, but he was equally certain that his mobile aid to law and crime would correct any fib. "Er... No. I have Jade Vernon with me," he said.

"I see." The words coming out of Malc were not delivered in the usual male monotone. The female voice emerging from him carried an element of opinion and it sounded to Luke like disapproval. "Never mind. Your mobile tells us you're in Sheffield. This is convenient."

"Oh?"

The Authorities had hijacked the mobile robot's synthetic speech circuitry to talk to Luke. "We are assigning you to a case of possible corruption there. It has come to our attention that a couple in Sheffield may have been paired inappropriately and unconventionally."

Puzzled, Luke frowned and glanced at the silent Jade.

"At least one member of the local Pairing Committee may have been unduly influenced."

Luke could not resist interrupting. "Influenced? What does that mean?"

At once, Malc's neutral male voice returned for a few seconds. "Persuaded, often by secret or unfair use of position; affected or altered by indirect or subtle means; swayed to modify the condition, development or outcome of something."

"Thanks, Malc," Luke muttered sarcastically. "Everything's a lot clearer now."

The voice of The Authorities continued, "I'm downloading all relevant notes to your mobile aid to law and crime. It's up to you to find out what form the influence takes, whether a committee member has succumbed to such pressure and, if so, who it is. If it's more than one member, it's your job to find out how many are involved and to identify them."

"But..."

"What?"

Luke could not admit to his doubts. He hated Pairing Committees. After all, they stood between him and a lifetime paired with Jade. If there was a way around the system of making life partners, he would rather celebrate than investigate it. But he was an FI. It was his duty to uphold the law. He could not pick and choose the rules he'd enforce. "I... um... I've only ever taken on murder cases."

"And you've done exceptionally well. This investigation is easier and lower profile. Think of it as a reward. After all," she added, "a change is as good as a rest." Her attempt at friendliness and informality came across as sinister.

"Do I have a choice?" Luke asked as he gazed into Jade's disbelieving face.

"No. Being in Sheffield, you're ideal for the job."

Luke swallowed. "There's something else," he said nervously.

"What's that?" the voice of The Authorities asked, clearly irritated that Luke dared to bring up another matter.

"It's... er... the case of Everton Kohter. He's scheduled for execution in two or three weeks. I want to look into it. You know. Just to make sure."

"Is this a serious request, FI Harding?"

"Yes."

"We do not raise doubts in the law without a very good reason."

"The good reason is, you could kill someone who's not done anything wrong. He was supposed to have murdered someone two years back. But mobiles have improved a lot since then. There's no harm in checking he's guilty with up-to-date methods."

There were a few moments of hesitation. "There is harm. It lies in reducing confidence in the law. Besides, I have now got the Kohter file on my monitor. The case against him is utterly watertight. He was arrested within minutes. I'd go as far as to say no one's ever been more clearly guilty of murder."

Luke had been tipped off by a mutual friend called Owen Goode that Kohter was not the killing kind so he decided not to cave in. "There's no problem getting a second opinion, then. I'll agree, and Kohter will be put to death knowing everything's been double-checked."

Malc's speech centre fell silent for a minute. Then the female voice sounded again. "We have granted your request. Reluctantly. I'll download all case notes to your mobile."

"Thanks," Luke replied. "Can you give him holographic programming, as well? I'll want him to recreate the crime scene so I can take a virtual walk through it and get a good look."

"Agreed, but I promise you won't have to be thorough to verify this verdict. And you won't need long but, for obvious reasons, you have nineteen days – until dawn on Sunday the twelfth of February. Kohter's execution will not be delayed."

The link to The Authorities broken, Jade stared at Luke. It wasn't often that she was lost for words. It wasn't for long either. "Inappropriate pairing?" she exclaimed. "Was that for real?"

"Sounds like it's my job to find out."

"Huh. There's more going on than that. They know about you and me." She nodded towards the robot that hovered beside Luke. "Malc tells them. He's probably telling them what we're saying now."

"Incorrect. Your current conversation is not relevant to either investigation."

"It might be in a second," Jade retorted. "They know we'd jump at the chance of inappropriate and unconventional pairing, so why give you the case?"

Not wanting to reveal his fears, Luke shrugged.

It was Malc who put Luke's suspicions into words. "Your loyalty to the law may be under test."

Luke looked at his mobile. "Do you know that? Have you been told that's what's going on?"

"No. It is a matter of logical deduction. Another explanation is that you are available and suitably located."

Luke smiled wryly. He expected that his mobile's obligation to the law, to the truth, and to himself would also come under test, and into conflict, before he got to the bottom of any illicit pairing. What concerned him more, though, was the looming execution of Everton Kohter.

Chapter Two

Rowan Pearce had been stabbed to death in the living room of his own home two years previously. The mobile aid to law and crime attending the scene had taken a standard three-dimensional laser scan of the interior of the London house and several views of the outside. Now, all of that information had been downloaded into Malc and he was ready to recreate it.

The local authorities in Sheffield had provided Luke with their huge emptied conference hall for the morning. It was here that Malc projected a virtual version of the murder scene. He erected two of Rowan Pearce's rooms within City Hall, like pitching a scruffy tent in lavish surroundings. The image was an exact reproduction, complete with furnishings, body, and stains. In this version, though, Luke and Malc could not touch anything because none of it was real. Luke did not have to wear gloves or worry about contaminating the evidence.

It was Rowan's body on the bare floorboards that first grabbed Luke's attention. It was so lifelike yet actually insubstantial. Luke reached down with his hand. If it had been a real corpse, he would have brushed Rowan's cold face, but it was just an optical illusion – like a mirage – so his fingers penetrated the man's skull. Luke shivered at the eerie sensation of reaching into a victim's head.

"If only I could pluck the last memories out of his brain," he said to himself. Those final images would have told him straightaway whether Everton Kohter or someone else had wielded the knife.

Rowan Pearce was twenty-six and his limbs were splayed out across the uncarpeted floor. Blood leaking from one stomach wound and two gashes in his chest had followed the lines of his body so that he appeared to be lying on a dark red star. The expression frozen on his lifeless face was one of surprise and shock. The knife, taken from the rack in the kitchen, was lying a couple of metres away.

Fascinated by the flimsy shell of a man, Luke inserted his hand into one of the chest wounds. "They must have done a full analysis of these injuries. Angles, depths and so on."

"They were consistent with Everton Kohter's height, physical strength and handedness."

Pointing at Rowan's trousers, Luke asked, "What's that stain?"

"Urine."

"Urine? Rowan's, I assume. Sometimes, a scare does that."

Malc replied, "It did not belong to the victim. DNA analysis gave a perfect match with Everton Kohter."

"It's Kohter's?" Luke's face crinkled into a grimace. "Ugh."

"In ancient times," Malc informed him, "warriors would urinate on their victims to emphasise their superiority."

"But you can't dent the deads' dignity. They're dead."

"It was believed to have a demoralizing effect on any enemy watching, and gave the victor a feeling of triumph."

"Mmm." For a moment, Luke felt regret. "I know almost everything about the law and almost nothing about history."

"That was inevitable from Year 8 when you chose to dedicate yourself to studying law and crime."

"Yeah. I guess." Squatting down near the pretend corpse, he examined Rowan's left hand. "Is this a bite mark?"

"Confirmed. The indentations matched the prime suspect's teeth."

Luke's sharp eyes spotted a small white stain on the victim's left shirt sleeve. "And this?"

"What is the nature of your query?"

"What is it?"

"It was saliva and DNA fingerprinting confirmed that it belonged to Everton Kohter."

"In ancient times, did warriors stress their superiority by spitting on their victims as well?"

"Confirmed."

"Charming." To stop Malc responding, Luke put up a

hand. "That's what we humans call tongue in cheek."

Malc hesitated while he referred to his dictionary. "Expressing the opposite of the intended literal meaning. Therefore, I conclude that you find expectoration distasteful."

"If that means spitting, yeah. But I suppose it's not as bad as murdering someone." Luke stood upright and looked around. In places, wallpaper was peeling away from cracked plasterwork. There was an upended chair, a table lying on its side and several scattered and broken ornaments. "There was a struggle," he said aloud. "Tell me about fingerprints."

"Fingerprints are the unique patterns left behind…"

Luke rolled his eyes because Malc had done this to him before. "I mean, tell me about the prints in here."

"The patterns on the kitchen knife were smeared but they almost certainly belonged to Everton Kohter, the victim, and his wife, Camilla Bunker. His partner's fingerprints were not considered significant for two reasons. First, she owned and used the knife. In addition, she died five days before his murder."

"How?"

"Her aeroplane crashed, killing all passengers and crew."

Luke nodded. "Were Kohter's prints anywhere else?"

"Confirmed."

"Where, then?"

The hovering robot highlighted each virtual location in turn with a red glow. "The overturned chair, the table, the door..."

"He wasn't careful and he didn't wear gloves, then," Luke interrupted with a smile.

"Correct."

"Did he leave any other evidence? What about the two muddy footprints over there by the front door?"

"They matched the shoes he was wearing. Flakes of dandruff on the floor also belonged to him. He left two hairs on the victim's clothing. His sweat was detected in several locations, especially the floor. Fibres from his clothes were found on a table leg and some floorboards, snagged on rough wood."

"Were they under the victim's fingernails as well?"

"No."

"How about skin?"

"Clarify your inquiry."

"Was Everton Kohter's skin found under Rowan's nails? When there's a struggle, the attacker's skin and fibres almost always end up under the victim's nails."

"In this case, no such evidence was found."

"Mmm. Interesting." Luke paused before asking, "Did Everton Kohter ever confess?"

"No."

"Did he deny it?"

"No. He claimed that he did not remember."

Luke was amazed. Almost everyone denied it, at least until they realized that the evidence was beyond doubt. "When and where was he arrested?"

"Approximately thirty-one minutes after the death. He remained outside the building."

Luke turned towards Malc in disbelief. "He hung around?"

Malc hesitated. "If hanging around is defined as lingering outside, you are correct."

"Where exactly?"

"Under an elm tree, five metres from the front door."

Luke shook his head and muttered, "Strange." Squinting at the false floorboards, he asked, "Are there bloodied footprints? Is that what I'm seeing?"

"Correct." Malc adjusted the hologram to mimic the effect of a laser scan in a darkened room and the footprints glowed an unearthly blue. "The trail was composed of the victim's blood and it led from the corpse to the prime suspect outside."

"What evidence was found on him?"

Malc adjusted the lighting so that the room appeared normal again to human eyes. "Everton Kohter had several bruises that he couldn't account for, one of the victim's hairs on his coat, and trousers soiled with urine. His hands and clothing were stained with substantial quantities of the victim's blood."

"Were the bloodstains consistent with someone who'd

just done this?" Luke indicated the stab wounds.

"Not recorded."

"Well, let's check. I want to see the pattern of blood stains on Everton Kohter."

Malc replied, "The finer points were considered irrelevant, given the strength of the case against the accused."

"I still want it."

"Task logged. I will re-examine the images of the culprit's clothing when my systems are not fully occupied with recreating the scene."

"What was his motive?"

"Temporary insanity."

Luke grunted. "I can see he went mad in here. And he must've been crazy to hang around afterwards." He thought about the muddy footprints for a moment before adding, "Was it raining at the time?"

"Searching case notes."

Luke wandered around the pretend living room. At the far end was a door and, out of habit, he reached out for the handle. Smiling, he stopped himself. In a dream house, he had no need to open doors and he could not grasp a make-believe handle anyway. He walked through the holographic wood as if he were parting a mist. Beyond it, the kitchen had been suspended in time like a spooky painting.

Following him, Malc said, "In London, the day of the murder was described as stormy."

"Well, I've never known a murderer shelter outside the crime scene, waiting for the rain to stop."

"Do you want me to search all criminal databases for examples when I have spare resource?"

Luke laughed. "No. It just doesn't happen."

On the worn work surface, stainless steel handles poked up out of the knife rack but one was missing.

"What about traces here?"

"What do you wish to know?"

Luke sighed and spelled it out. "What trace evidence was found here and what were the deductions?"

"There was no useful evidence," Malc answered. "The fingerprints belonged only to the house owners. One pattern was rejected because it was marked, but it was still identifiable as belonging to Camilla Bunker."

Luke wafted his hand through the virtual knives. There was no friction, no sharpness, no pain. No substance at all. "Is this a heavy base? Could someone grab a knife in one hand and just pull it out? If they had to hold the base down, there'd be prints on it as well as the handle."

"Insufficient data. The case notes do not include this detail."

"Check it, please."

"Logged," Malc replied.

"Was there any evidence that Everton Kohter had come in here at all? Any more muddy footprints?"

"No."

"His fingerprints weren't on the door or handle?"

"No."

"He was careless enough to leave prints on the front door but not on this one. That's weird."

Malc was never surprised. He merely deduced. "It would suggest that the kitchen door was wide open."

Luke was dubious. "If Rowan was in the living room, you're saying he let Everton wander past into the kitchen and grab a knife!" Strolling back through the virtual door like a ghost, Luke asked, "What was the link between Everton Kohter and the victim? Did they know each other?"

Malc answered, "It was a random attack. That is not uncommon in cases of temporary insanity."

"Were there any finds that didn't point to Everton Kohter?"

"No."

"Were there traces of anyone in here apart from Kohter, the victim and his partner?"

"No."

Again, Luke squatted by the copy of Rowan Pearce's body. "What was his life like, Malc? And his relationships."

"Not recorded. It was considered irrelevant to the case."

The smile on Luke's face was ironic. He thought that the lives of the dead were always relevant. He stood up again and surveyed the room for the last time. "How exactly did Kohter get in? He didn't walk through the wood like I can."

"The prisoner claimed that the door was slightly open. It was assumed that he simply pushed it and entered."

Luke frowned. "It was open in a storm?"

"Correct."

Luke halted with his hands on his hips. "Well, what can I say?" He glanced at Malc. "No, don't answer that. A few things don't make sense but…" He shrugged helplessly.

"In a case of insanity, you should not expect the culprit's behaviour to make sense. Otherwise he would not be insane."

Luke could not argue with his mobile's logic. "True."

Malc concluded, "There are no flaws in the case. The evidence is overwhelming. It is easily sufficient to charge Everton Kohter with the murder of Rowan Pearce."

Luke nodded sadly. "Easily enough to get him convicted and executed as well."

Chapter Three

Rowan Pearce's house dissolved in front of Luke's eyes. It was like waking up from a dream. Back in the real world, doors and walls were solid and Luke couldn't float through a crime scene with a sense of detachment from the cruelty. He blinked and then looked at Malc. "While I'm here, do the people on the Pairing Committee know I'm investigating them?"

"Your location is irrelevant. They do not know there is an investigation."

"No. I mean, while I'm in the same building as them, I could get things moving. Request a meeting, Malc."

The full Pairing Committee of four people could not be assembled at short notice but the Chairperson agreed to meet Luke in her office. About fifty years of age, Nicoletta Boniwell was an instructor as well as Chair of the committee. Along with her three colleagues, she supervised all pairings in the Sheffield area.

When every young person reached The Time – twenty years of age – Ms Boniwell and her team had the responsibility of making sure that they were coupled strictly according to the rules laid down by The Authorities. Pairs were formed on the basis of career, age, intelligence and genetics. A musician like Jade would be paired with an artist to produce artistically talented offspring. A forensic investigator would be coupled with a scientist. All partners had to be of the same age. Arranging or taking part in pairings outside of the rules was against the law.

Behind an imposing desk, Nicoletta Boniwell typed a few words on a keypad and then gazed at the screen.

Standing in front of her, Luke breathed the air that was richly scented with her perfume. He could not see her monitor, yet he could guess what she was reading.

She looked up at him with a puzzled frown. "Everything looks clear-cut in your file. You're to be matched with a girl called Georgia Bowie – a biologist." She waved her hand dismissively, flashing a pairing ring decorated with a large sapphire.

Luke hesitated, working out how best to protest and, without making it obvious that he was conducting an inquiry, discover if the committee would consider an illegal pairing. Before he could reply, Malc interrupted.

"Officially," the mobile said, "Luke Harding and Georgia Bowie's pairing has not been confirmed. The committee in London was attacked before it could ratify the arrangement."

Luke knew that Malc was simply reporting the truth – as his programming always required – but he liked to think that the mobile was on his side, doing what he could to resist the system.

Nicoletta Boniwell studied her screen for a while

longer and then said, "That seems to be correct. What do you want? Are you asking us to approve the pairing?"

"No," Luke replied. He decided to be blunt. After all, he was a forensic investigator on a case of possible corruption and he wanted to lay a trap for the Pairing Committee. "I'm asking you to change it. I'm hoping you'll pair me with Jade Vernon."

The woman looked shocked. She turned away from him and coughed gruffly into her hand. "This is extremely unusual, FI Harding. Pairing Committees do not consider requests. They decide what's best for the future. Your mobile will remind you of the reasoning."

"Research has shown that the early stages of romantic love are merely a driving force like hunger or thirst. They do not involve emotional centres of the brain. Rather, the human brain is simply pursuing a pleasurable reward, like eating chocolate. Such urgent pleasurable need is called lust. Later in a relationship, the brain recovers from obsession and forms a longer lasting bond involving its emotional centres. The pairing system stops young people engaging in impulsive and unwise couplings in pursuit of pleasure. By imposing rational unions, Pairing Committees aim for long-term commitment directly. They also consider genetic compatibility for childbearing. The purpose of pairing is to produce children with specific desired skills."

To Luke, Malc sounded not such a friend this time. In

trying to get himself paired with Jade, Luke was on his own.

"Just because you're an investigator," Nicoletta continued, "you don't get special treatment." Her eyes flitted to her monitor again. "Besides, isn't Jade Vernon a musician here in Sheffield?"

"Yes."

"There's your answer, then. She's to be paired with an artist."

"I'm not asking for special treatment," Luke replied. "I'm just asking for a bit of... lateral thinking." He remembered that Jade had once called herself an assistant forensic investigator because she'd used her talent with sound to help him out in two cases. She was only joking, Luke knew, but she'd given him a new angle. "Jade's a musician but she's scientifically minded and technically competent. She's played a vital role in two of my cases. In effect, she's my assistant when it comes to using and analysing sound. Confirm, please, Malc."

At once, Malc agreed. "Her command of acoustics assisted in the arrest of one suspect and her analysis of footsteps provided a strong lead in a second murder investigation. I can retrieve the relevant files if required."

Ms Boniwell ignored Malc and gazed at Luke. "Basically she's a musician. An artist."

"Her knack for science might be suppressed most of the time but it's there," Luke replied. "That means our genes are compatible."

"All right, FI Harding." Nicoletta shuffled uncomfortably and leaned forwards, dangling the long fingers of her right hand over the front edge of the desk. "I'll reflect on what you've said, even if it is irregular. The committee will speak to Jade Vernon but we won't contact your intended partners until we've reached a conclusion. I'll call you to an interview in due course. But, if I were you, I wouldn't hold out much hope."

Staring at Owen Goode's face on his telescreen, Luke shrugged. "I've seen the evidence now, Owen. Short of writing 'This is the work of Everton Kohter' all over the wall in the victim's blood, your mate's guilty. I'm sorry. He even spat and peed on the body. And bit it. That's not what normal, innocent people do. His sweat, hair, and fibres from his clothes were all over the place. He left behind enough evidence to prove himself guilty four times over. When the FI found him, he was outside the victim's house, dazed, covered in bruises, with the victim's blood splashed over him."

"I don't believe it."

"There was a trail of blood from the body to where he was standing."

Owen shook his head obstinately. "Go and speak to him. Then decide."

Luke let out a long breath. "It won't do any good. Not when he's buried in an avalanche of evidence."

"But you don't know him."

It was true. He was condemning Everton without even meeting him. The life of a suspect was just as relevant as that of a victim. "All right," Luke said. "I'll go. But..."

"Yeah. I know. Likely, you can't promise anything."

"More than that. I can't think what could possibly overturn that amount of forensic evidence."

Chapter Four

Jade hit the Save button and whipped off her headphones, making her unruly hair even more disarrayed. She'd had it dyed so it was a chaos of brilliant colour, ready to startle the nightclubbers at her gig tonight. With a grin, she said, "Hiya. How's tricks?"

"I've... er... got some bad news," Luke replied, eager to get it over with.

"Oh? What's that?" she asked, still sitting at the terminal of her mixer, headphones dangling from her right hand.

"I've got to go to Cambridge tomorrow."

"Cambridge?" she exclaimed. "Yuck. Why?"

"Sorry, but I've got to interview a prisoner – the one who's up for the death penalty."

"Let's see." Jade stroked her chin theatrically. "A nightclub in Sheffield with me or a Cambridge prison with a murderer. Mmm. That's a tricky choice you've got."

"All right. All right. I'd rather stay here with you but..."

"You could interview him by telescreen."

"Yeah, but it's not the same," Luke replied. "Face-to-face is best for what I've got to do."

"If you did it by telescreen, you could come to my gig."

Luke sighed. "You could stream your stuff to Malc. I can listen that way."

Jade looked horrified. "That's not the same either. Face-to-face is the only way. You've got to be there, hear it live. And you need a decent sound system."

Luke paused and then said, "You're going to be great, I know. You're going to give everyone a real good time. I'm jealous. But, at the end of the day, you're into entertaining people, Jade, and I've got to double-check the death sentence given to a fifteen-year-old. Thirteen at the time of the murder." He shrugged. "If he's innocent, I've got just over two weeks to do the impossible."

"What?"

"Dig him out from under a mountain of evidence."

"And you've got this crazy Pairing Committee job as well."

Luke had not yet looked into the details of the illicit couple because Everton Kohter's predicament was more important and urgent. Luke intended to interview them after his Cambridge trip. "Yes," he said, blushing. "That's another thing."

"What is?"

"You might get hauled in front of the committee."

Jade frowned. "Me? Why?"

Telling her what he'd said to Nicoletta Boniwell felt like a confession.

Jade's hand froze in her hair. "What are you trying to do, Luke? Get paired with me or are you playing the FI, laying a trap for them?"

Luke took a deep breath. "Both, I suppose."

Jade let out a snort. "No chance! If they say no, you haven't got a case of corruption and you're not paired with me. If they say yes, you've either got a case against them or you get us paired. You can't have it both ways."

"If they say yes, we might have to go through with it. Get them to ratify our pairing. You know, to make sure they're willing to bend the system."

"But then they're guilty and The Authorities will quash it."

"Not if I can make them look innocent."

Jade threw up her hands. "Much as I like the idea, I can't see it happening. You're a dreamer, Luke." Her frown turned into a smile as she said, "But I like you for it."

Briefly, Luke's electric cab ran alongside Rutland Water. The bank was encrusted with frost and large plates of ice still floated on the lake, but most of it had thawed. A little light snow began to drift down from a heavy sky, reflecting Luke's mood.

There was a gulf between the north and the south but no clear dividing line. As the cab skirted around Peterborough, the countryside began to look unkempt and many of the houses were in poor repair. Watching the worsening living conditions, Luke did not relish his return to the south but he was curious about the young prisoner awaiting his appointment with the Death Cell.

"Not far from Cambridge," Luke said sadly.

"Forty-seven point two kilometres from the prison," Malc informed him.

"Tell them when I'll arrive and who I'm coming to see."

"Transmitting."

"Play me the sound clip of Everton Kohter's arrest, please."

Malc located the file in a matter of seconds and activated it. The clear voice of a forensic investigator stood out from the background noise. "You're in serious trouble, Kohter. I ask you again. How did you get this blood all over you?"

A quiet and confused thirteen-year-old voice responded, "Don't know."

Behind the talk was the constant patter of rain.

"Shall I tell you? You stabbed him. Three times. Why?"

There was no answer. But there was another sound. It could have been the sniff of someone trying to suppress sobs.

"You've got his blood on your shoes," the FI said. "It doesn't take much figuring out, does it?"

"Don't know," Everton repeated.

The boy made the same noise again. It didn't sound like an attempt to hold back tears this time. Luke wasn't sure what it was.

"Everton Kohter. I have sufficient evidence to charge you with the murder of Rowan Pearce."

Then something happened that astounded Luke. The strangled noise escaped from Everton's throat and it became a laugh. Facing a murder conviction and the death penalty if found guilty, Everton laughed loud and long.

Plainly the FI was amazed at the time as well. "What's funny, Kohter?" he snapped, the anger obvious in his tone.

But Everton seemed to find the whole thing too hilarious to answer. He must have been doubled up with laughter.

Shocked, Luke said to Malc, "Thanks. That's enough. I know why it was put down to madness now."

"Throughout further questioning, the prisoner laughed frequently and inappropriately."

Luke shook his head. "Weird."

"I have traced the manufacturer of the set of kitchen knives in the victim's house. The base is one point eight kilograms, designed to be heavy enough to allow the withdrawal of a knife without holding down the rack. This information is consistent with the killer's fingerprints appearing only on the knife and not elsewhere in the kitchen."

"What about the blood stains on Everton Kohter? Do they match the spatter pattern you'd expect for someone who'd made those three stab wounds?"

"No. The smears suggest that the culprit rolled in the blood."

Luke turned up his nose. "Why does someone kill, spit

and pee on his victim, roll around in the blood and then laugh his head off?"

"It is impossible for laughter to cause decapitation," Malc replied. "But the first four activities are indicative of an unbalanced mind."

"Yeah," said Luke. Other than that, he was lost for words.

Chapter Five

Whenever Luke got out of a cab, he would always survey his surroundings. It was particularly important to glance around in the south where bandits might be lying in wait. This time, when the automated vehicle came to a halt outside Block J of Cambridge Prison, his eyes locked on to the imposing prison building and, for a moment, he froze. Captivated, he did not take in anything else.

Beyond the strong iron gate, a straight walkway led to the reinforced entrance to the grim building. On either side of the path there were tall brick walls with coils of fearsome razor wire on top, making the approach to the prison seem like a dark tunnel. The block was built of plain stone that had blackened over time and the main door was set within a forbidding concrete arch. Luke could see armed guards high up on the turrets at the front corners.

Taking a deep breath, he swiped his identity card through the reader. Normally, any door would spring open for a forensic investigator, but not here in Cambridge. A voice told him to keep still and to avoid blinking while a laser in the gatepost performed an iris scan to prove his identity.

After a few seconds, the gate lifted up vertically, allowing him to enter the oppressive channel. Behind him, the iron barrier slid back down and banged shut with a clunk that sounded final. Only the most hardened criminals – and all inmates sentenced to death – were sent to Block J. Four guards would escort a prisoner approaching the intimidating door: two in front and two behind. But Luke went uneasily along the pathway with only Malc for company. He wondered how Everton had coped with this short walk towards a bleak building that he would never leave.

Within a few metres of the massive entrance, the sound of Luke's footsteps changed noticeably. He was walking on a hollow surface. He shuddered as he realized that he was going over a drawbridge with water below. In the event of an emergency, this part of the walkway could be hauled upright and the block isolated by a deep moat that encircled the building as if it were an ancient castle.

At the door there was another reader. Luke passed his identity card over it and the huge arched door creaked open, revealing the Superintendent and three armed guards in a large reception like the mouth of a cave.

The prison Superintendent stepped forwards and welcomed Luke without enthusiasm. "FI Harding. You're younger than I... Anyway, come in. I must say it's very unusual for someone like you to visit one of my inmates. By the time they've come under my wing, you've normally finished with them."

Inside, Luke shivered. He didn't reply.

35

"We've got Kohter in our interview room, ready for you. Can I ask you why…?"

The unsettling thud of the door shutting interrupted the end of his question.

Luke kept his answer brief. "I'm conducting a check on the evidence against him."

"Really?"

"Confirm, Malc."

"A review of this case has been sanctioned prior to execution."

Surprised, the Superintendent echoed the opinion of The Authorities. "It won't take long." He paused before explaining, "I know what Kohter's done has got nothing to do with me. I just carry out what the law dictates, but I looked into his case. I guess because he's my youngest prisoner. There's no doubt he's guilty."

Luke shrugged. "Looks like it."

"I can tell you don't want to discuss it with me – why should you? – but… Anyway, my staff will take you to him. Are you carrying any weapons?"

Luke shook his head. "Never."

"All right. There'll be two guards outside at any time. If necessary, you can call…"

Luke sighed. "It won't come to that. Malc has defensive capabilities."

"Even so…"

"Has Kohter ever been violent?" asked Luke.

"Strangely, no. But that doesn't mean…"

"Has he ever confessed while he's been here?"

"No."

"Okay. I'd like to see him straightaway."

Flanked by two guards and with Malc hovering behind, Luke went down two starkly lit and chillingly plain passageways until they came to a halt outside a door. When their loud footsteps fell silent, it was like a heart had stopped beating. One of the guards – a man called Greg Roper – unlocked the solid door and it slid slowly aside with a whirring noise.

Inside, a boy was sitting on a chair that was bolted into the floor. The only other pieces of furniture were a table and a second chair. The featureless walls were painted a soothing light green. With one wrist handcuffed to an arm of the chair, Everton looked up at his visitor but there was no trace of hope in his blank expression. He was scrawny, much shorter than Luke, and he looked incapable of harming anyone. His hair had been shorn, revealing the remnant of an old wound – a purple stripe on light brown skin – above his right ear. It was his eyes that Luke noticed most. There was nothing there. No depth. No sparkle. No life.

The bare room contrasted with Jade's slick apartment in Sheffield and Luke's hotel suite, partly converted into an office and mini-laboratory for an FI's use. Both were pure luxury compared to this anonymous interview room. Overwhelmed by the depressing atmosphere, Luke asked Greg Roper to remove Everton's handcuff.

"I can't do that, sir. Regulations."

Apparently confused by the investigator's request, the boy gazed at Luke in silence.

"A drink, then. Do you want one, Everton?"

Before Everton could answer, the prison guard said, "I can bring you something, sir, but not…"

"All right," Luke replied. "Pomegranate juice. But it's been a long journey. I'm very thirsty. Bring me two glasses, please." Before Roper had a chance to object, Luke turned towards Everton and said bluntly, "Did you do it?"

Everton cocked his head on one side. He stared at Luke for a second, then dropped his gaze. "Don't know."

With those two words, Everton Kohter went a long way to convincing FI Harding that he was innocent. When the guilty claimed to be innocent, they always answered that question with a simple and certain, "No." Culprits never tried to escape the punishment of the law by declaring that they didn't know whether they'd committed a crime or not.

"My name's Luke. I've been asked to check your case out," he said. "And I'm a friend of Owen Goode. He's thinking about you."

"Owen," the boy murmured as if he'd been isolated from the outside world for so long that he could no longer bring his mates and old haunts to mind.

"You know what hit me when I looked through your file? You never said, 'I didn't do it.' Not when you were arrested. Not under questioning. Not once did you claim you're innocent."

"You're a forensic investigator."

Luke nodded. "Why didn't you deny it?"

Everton shrugged. "Can't remember what I did."

"Do you think you're capable of murdering someone?"

He sniffed and thought about it as if no one had ever bothered to ask him before. "I guess... No, not really, but the FI went through all the evidence against me."

He appeared worn down. Maybe, within these miserable walls, all of his youthful optimism had been crushed out of him. Maybe the certainty of his execution had numbed his spirit. To all intents and purposes, he was dead even before he began the final walk to the Death Cell, flanked by a couple of guards. At least that way, he'd feel no pain and no regret. He'd feel nothing.

Greg Roper came back into the cell with two plastic cups of a deep red juice. He placed them on the table and said to Luke, "They're both for you."

"Thanks," Luke said, picking up the first cup and draining it. "That's good."

As soon as the door closed, Luke pushed the second drink towards the boy's free hand. "Want it? It's great. My favourite."

Everton stared at the juice suspiciously before glancing up at Luke. Then his fingers shot out like a striking snake. He grabbed the drink, gulped it down in one and licked his lips.

"What do you remember about that day, two years ago?"

"I... don't know. I was walking. Heard a noise. Don't know what. Maybe a voice or something. It was raining. I went up to this house. I could see the door was open. It was dark and then... Nothing. It's all blank. Next thing was being arrested."

Luke nodded. "Why did you hang around outside the house for half an hour afterwards?"

"Didn't know I'd done anything wrong. Why should I run away?"

"Strange the door was open in the rain. Was it wide open?"

Everton closed his dull eyes. "No. Just a bit."

"What did you mean when you said it was dark? The house was dark?"

Everton shook his head helplessly.

He wasn't behaving like a suspect who was trying to hide something. He seemed genuinely unable to answer. He wasn't behaving like the guilty either. He didn't grumble about being questioned, he made more eye contact than a culprit usually did, and he didn't try to blame someone else for the crime.

"How come you were going past his house?"

"I'd run out of school to get away from... kids who were having a go at me. Not for the first time. Just needed a break. I was walking back."

"So, you were angry at the time."

Everton shook his head. "Sad."

"Was it raining? Didn't you get soaked?"

Everton looked away while he thought about it. "Not sure. Not at first. Maybe it came down when I got to the house." He shrugged his slim shoulders.

"Did you know Rowan Pearce?"

"No."

Luke changed his tactics. "Why did you spit on him?"

"Did I? Don't remember."

"What did the kitchen look like?"

"No idea," Everton answered.

"Have you ever suffered blackouts?"

"No."

"When you were arrested, you laughed. And again under questioning. Frequently and inappropriately, according to the notes. It didn't go down well. Why did you do that?"

"I couldn't help it."

Luke gazed at him for a few seconds and then turned to Malc. "Define hysterical, please."

Malc replied, "One: extremely funny. Two: suffering an unmanageable emotional outburst characterized by fits of laughing or weeping."

41

"Which were you, Everton? Hilarious, or were you panic-stricken and out of control?"

"Looking back, it wasn't funny, was it? Not for me, not for Mr Pearce."

"So, it *was* an emotional outburst. Why didn't you deny killing Rowan Pearce? Why don't you now?"

Everton wiped his mouth with his loose hand. "How can I? Seems like I did. But it doesn't matter any more, does it?"

"How do you mean?"

Everton's dead eyes focused on him. "They're going to execute me pretty soon."

Luke nodded slowly. "If you want my help to try and stop it, you've got to think back and give me something I can use."

For several seconds, Everton seemed to make a real attempt to recall something, then he shrugged again. His long stay in prison had broken him.

"Did you see anyone else, inside or outside the house?"

"I can't remember knifing him, spitting, getting covered in blood. Nothing. So, I'm not going to remember anyone running away." He didn't raise his voice. He wasn't cross. He was merely confused and frustrated.

"I didn't say anything about running away. Did you see someone running away, Everton?"

"Don't think so."

"All right. I'm going in a bit. Are you sure you can't tell me anything?"

Everton shook his head.

"Okay. I'll try and get you out of this anyway," Luke promised. As he got up, he added, "If you think of anything – anything at all – tell a guard."

"Yeah. But I'm not going to. Not after all this time."

Luke gazed into his face again. "You're doing pretty good, under the circumstances. Very calm."

"As good as dead."

"I'm sorry. It must be very hard for you," Luke replied sympathetically.

Everton shook his head. "It's not hard to be dead."

Chapter Six

Alongside the track was a long line of wind turbines. Beyond them, the Midlands raced past. Alone in the warm cab, Luke imagined a heavy sword dangling over Everton Kohter. With each passing hour, the sharp blade dropped a little further, getting closer and closer. So far, Luke had nothing to halt its descent.

Of course, he wasn't really alone in the cab. An FI was hardly ever truly alone. He had his permanent companion with him. He asked Malc to establish a sound-only link to Owen Goode. It took half an hour, though, because Owen was busy in Greenwich clearing up the old domed warehouse that the Thames had flooded. He was intent on turning the place into a school for sport. He wouldn't call it a school, though, because he hated schools and the demands of instructors. Besides, the children who were drawn to him had already run away from one school. They wouldn't willingly go to another.

"I've been to see your mate in Cambridge," Luke said into the air. "Everton."

Malc relayed Luke's words to London, received the response, and regenerated Owen's voice using his speech synthesis program.

"And?" Owen prompted.

Luke avoided the question. "Tell me about him. What

makes you so sure he's innocent?"

"I just know. He's not the type. Not a bit of violence in him."

Luke did not give up. "But what makes you think like that?"

"Well, I suppose there *is* something," Owen's voice replied. "It was ages ago, when we were both at school together. I never got on with instructors. He never got on with kids. Always a weedy guy, he didn't like sport. Likely, that's why some of the others picked on him. He was only interested in running – running away. And he didn't do that very well. Anyway, two lads went for him. It was obvious what was going to happen. Everton had a javelin in his hand and he was right by a rack with lots more. He was hopeless with a javelin but he still could've speared them both before they laid a finger on him. Could have done them a lot of damage. But he didn't do anything to protect himself. Took quite a beating instead."

"What did you do?"

"Me? I'm not shy about using a javelin when I have to." He laughed at the memory. "Prodded them both, like. Nothing too serious. Just enough to scare them off. Champion."

"Maybe the whole thing taught Everton to get his attack in first next time. Maybe it turned him violent."

"No chance. Not Everton."

"All right, Owen. Thanks a lot. I'm working on it."

"But you don't give him much hope, do you?"

Luke hesitated and then replied glumly, "Even *he* thinks he's guilty."

Turning his mind back to his investigation of the irregular pairing in Sheffield as he approached the city, Luke said, "If the members of the committee get to know they're being investigated, they're not going to fall into my trap. They'd be on their best behaviour till I clear them. So, I can't interview them without letting on that I'm on their tails."

"Human beings do not possess..."

Luke sighed. "On their tails means chasing them. Enter into dictionary."

"Logged," Malc said obediently.

"Anyway, I could talk to the couple who've been paired but shouldn't have been, according to The Authorities."

"You have been cleared to interview Mollie Gazzo and Rufus Vile."

"Check they're available, Malc, then program the cab to take me to them. And tell me why their pairing's wrong."

"The Authorities' records indicate that Mollie Gazzo is four years older than Rufus Vile. This contravenes the age requirement for pairing."

"The Pairing Committee knew this?"

"Ms Boniwell denied it. Mollie Gazzo had recently

moved to Sheffield and her identity card, which the committee checked, recorded her age as twenty years. If this had been correct, she would have been the same age as Rufus Vile."

Luke was perplexed. "You mean, there was a mistake on her identity card? I've never heard of that before. I thought it was impossible."

"It appears there was an error in the memory chip."

It was dark outside but Sheffield's floodlit Southern Park was still eye-catching. It was a beautiful mixture of evergreens, lush lawns, a swimming pool, sports fields, an animal sanctuary, and lakes. Some people from the city were walking through it for leisure, others were jogging for fitness or engaged in organized sport, and a few children were playing as the snow drifted down again.

"So, why's the Pairing Committee in the firing line? I mean, why are they getting blamed? Isn't it the card's fault?"

"It is standard practice to check The Authorities' files before any pairing is confirmed."

Luke glanced at Malc and shrugged. "Sounds more like someone cutting corners than corruption."

"Explain."

"Maybe they just did a sloppy job. Maybe they didn't intend to break the rules. They relied on the identity card, thinking it was a waste of time to check files."

"The Authorities believe that a committee member

consulted their records but ignored the information and continued with an illegal pairing."

"Ah," Luke replied. "Which committee member?"

"Unknown. It was someone using a computer within Sheffield City Hall. The task would normally be undertaken by the Chairperson."

"What about Mollie Gazzo's identity card? Was it a deliberate mistake – a forgery – or just a bug in the electronic system?"

"Unknown. Clarifying the status of the identity card should form part of your investigation."

The cab shifted onto tracks that led to the southwest of the city. Luke turned to Malc where he rested on the seat, plugged into the cab's energy port to recharge his battery. "Where are we going?"

"Burbage Rocks. I have confirmed that Mollie Gazzo and Rufus Vile are available at the geothermal power station, where they have both just started the night shift. They are expecting you."

"They're technologists?"

"Correct."

The cab slowed as it hit the sharp gradient and climbed through Ringinglow Wood. Suddenly, the world beyond the automated vehicle became shadowy and sinister. As the cab rose above the tree line, the atmosphere changed. The bright lights of Sheffield appeared to Luke's right and a long way below him. He gazed at them through falling snow and then raised his eyes. The stars in the night sky were obscured by the blizzard but not quite hidden by whiteout. Soon, the silvery geothermal power station came into his view. Its three chimneys glinted in the station's exterior lights and a pillar of steam rose from each one.

Luke had never been inside a geothermal power station. He knew how they worked, though. It was a simple idea but the necessary engineering was complex. Cold water was driven five kilometres underground where the hot earth boiled it, turning it into superheated steam. The steam returned to the surface where it powered a turbine to make a large amount of Sheffield's electricity. Wind farms on the Peaks provided the rest.

The huge building was not as secure as Cambridge Prison. The large door was programmed to respond to the identity cards of its own staff, The Authorities and forensic investigators. It swung aside for Luke as soon as he swiped his card past the reader.

Inside, there was a steady drone. Somewhere within the building, gigantic steel wheels turned relentlessly. The whole place seemed to hum with the constant churning.

Mollie Gazzo and Rufus Vile were standing in the computer room in front of a panel of telescreens. Each one showed graphs, rows of figures, and a series of coloured lights as the giant processor monitored every aspect of the power station's performance. Occasionally, Mollie or Rufus would step forwards and make an adjustment by typing on a keypad but there wasn't a hint of panic. Everything seemed to be under control. Mollie was clearly a few years older than her husband.

Luke introduced himself and then said, "It doesn't really matter – you're not under any sort of suspicion – but I wondered how you two met. Was it here at work?"

Rufus and Mollie exchanged a worried glance. It was Mollie who answered. "No. I'm not from Sheffield. We met at a course on the information technology of power generation. It was in Derby." She stumbled over some of the words because she was sucking a sweet.

"And you got on well," Luke prompted.

They both nodded.

"Mmm," Luke muttered as he viewed the bank of telescreens. "Bit of a coincidence that you got paired."

Rufus coughed heavily, moved closer to Luke and pressed a couple of keys. "A happy coincidence," he stressed. "We're very pleased with how it worked out. Aren't we, Mollie?"

"Yes, Roof."

Luke sniffed silently. Rufus was wearing a lot of deodorant. Turning back to Mollie, he asked, "Did you move to Sheffield to be closer to Rufus?"

Noticing a packet of extra-strong mints lying by one of the keyboards, Mollie picked it up and slipped it into her pocket. The sapphire in her pairing ring caught for a moment on the cloth. "Er... yes. That's right."

"And did you try to influence the Pairing Committee?"

Again they looked at each other. This time, they both shook their heads in denial.

"You see," Luke continued, "it seems strange that it worked out. Especially when you're not as old as each other."

"Ah. There was a mix-up over our ages," Rufus replied, "but we didn't object."

"And you didn't point it out."

"No. Well, would you? We wanted to be paired."

Luke smiled. "No, if I wanted an illegal pairing, I wouldn't either. I'm no great fan of pairing rules." He paused before adding, "It was your identity card, wasn't it, Mollie?"

"Yes. There's an error on it."

"Mmm. How did that happen?"

She shrugged. "It says I'm twenty but I'm twenty-four really."

"I want my mobile to scan it, please."

Mollie shifted the sweet from one cheek to the other. "Do I have any choice?"

Smiling, Luke shook his head. "Sorry. None at all."

She was wearing it on a chain around her neck. She yanked it out from under her clothes and held it out for Malc to scan.

"Did you alter it in some way?" Luke asked. "You know about information technology."

"Nowhere near enough to bypass the security of an identity card. That's tough."

"Are there people who can do it?" asked Luke.

"I shouldn't think so."

"Pity," Luke replied. He took a deep breath as the other two gazed at him in shock. "To be honest, that's what this is all about. You see, I'm going to be paired with someone I'd rather not be paired with. And there's a girl I'm very keen on. Confirm, please, Malc."

"In the matter of pairing, FI Harding is considered uncooperative and undisciplined by The Authorities."

"So, if there's a way of altering an identity card or influencing the Sheffield Pairing Committee, I'd be... very interested."

Luke knew that he had not convinced them. There was distrust in their faces. Neither of them replied.

He let out a breath to show his frustration. "Telling me how you did it won't get you into any more trouble."

But there wasn't a murmur from either of them.

"All right. I'm done for now, but I'll be in touch. If you don't cooperate next time, I'll get heavy. I can arrest you for not answering my questions. Think about it." He left the room with Malc gliding behind him. As soon as he shut the door, he whispered, "I want you to take an air sample for analysis. They're covering something up with mints and perfume. Okay?"

"Logged."

When Luke banged on the door and went back in with Malc, the two technologists sprang apart like naughty schoolchildren. "I just want you to think how it'd feel if you hadn't been paired together. It'd hurt, wouldn't it? A lot. Well, that's how I feel right now." He glowered at them, venting his emotion. "So, I'm relying on you to understand and help me out. You know what I want. I'll see you soon." Then he left with a flourish.

Chapter Seven

As Luke strode back towards the main entrance, he said, "Well? You took an air sample. Are you doing the analysis?"

"Confirmed. However, it is a very complicated mixture. There are hundreds of trace components. I am attempting chromatographic separation and identifying as many airborne substances as possible."

"Hundreds? Why? That's not normal, is it?"

"No. It is an unusually complex sample. I am processing."

Outside, the night air had dropped a few more degrees and Luke shivered. He swiped his identity card through the corridor reader and said into the microphone, "Sheffield Hotel." The cab had not moved. Its door opened and Luke stepped gratefully into its warm interior. With a slight jolt, it began the long descent into the twinkling city that had spread itself over the picturesque bowl between the surrounding hills.

As the cab ran through the suburbs, Malc reported, "Apart from the known major components of air, I am detecting some unusual substances. Civetone, phenylethanal, menthol…"

Luke interrupted him. "I've heard of that one. Isn't menthol minty?"

"Correct. It is extracted from the peppermint plant or common mint herb."

"That'll be the sweets Mollie was keen to hide. What are the other two?"

"Civetone is a floral musky odour used in perfumes, originally obtained from an anal sac of the civet cat."

Luke squirmed in his seat. "It's from the wrong end of an animal and it's supposed to smell nice?"

"In concentrated form, it is said to be disagreeably pungent. Diluted, it is pleasing to humans and it has been used as a fragrance for over two thousand years."

"What's phenylethanal?"

"It is the odour of hyacinths, also used in perfumes."

"Okay. So far, you've got deodorants and mints. That's what they were using to cover something up. What else have you found?"

"Traces of benzene, pyrrolidine, dimethylamine and nicotine."

"Are they to do with a geothermal power station?"

"No. In that combination, I am aware of only one source. They are breakdown products of tobacco."

"Tobacco?" Luke replied. "Isn't that a plant?"

"Correct. It is any of the *Nicotiana* genus of the potato family with large sticky leaves and tubular flowers. Specifically, it refers to *Nicotiana tabacum* which is cultivated overseas for its leaves."

"Oh? What are they used for?"

"They are dried, cut and wrapped in thin paper to make the shape of a narrow cylinder called a cigarette.

This is set on fire and its smoke inhaled."

Luke grimaced. "Are you sure?"

"If there is uncertainty in any of my statements, I am required to make it clear."

"It sounds crazy."

"Smoking cigarettes in this country is illegal. It is harmful to human health, causing heart disease, lung cancer and other conditions."

"I'm not surprised it's illegal. Why would anyone do it?"

"Tobacco smoke contains thousands of substances. Some are said to aid relaxation and others are addictive."

"So," Luke deduced, "Mollie Gazzo and Rufus Vile have been smoking tobacco."

Malc agreed. "Highly likely."

"Good. That gives me something to use against them."

"As it is an illegal activity, you are obliged to investigate."

"That's right. I don't have enough cases on my hands already, do I?" Luke moaned.

The cab stopped and Luke made straight for the hotel reception.

Luke was lying on the bed, hands clasped behind his head, gazing at the night sky that Malc had projected onto the white ceiling. "Is it worth my while getting up in the morning?" Luke asked.

Malc hesitated. "Confirmed. But the purpose of your question is unclear."

"I mean, did you find a supply of pomegranates? It's hard to face the day without one for breakfast."

"I located an all-year-round supply from the Middle East. I have arranged import from Jordan."

"Brilliant. That's the power of an FI, put to good use." Luke paused for a moment and then asked, "If these tobacco leaves come from overseas, how do they get imported?"

"Details are not known with certainty, but they are smuggled by boat. Illegal consignments have also been seized by The Authorities from people flying into England."

Luke watched a shooting star, or at least the image of one. It was no more real than the hologram of Rowan Pearce's body and house. "Find an address for Rufus Vile and Mollie Gazzo. Tomorrow, I want to drop in on them. If they're using these dried leaves for smoking, there'll be particles in their house. You can suck up a sample of dust for analysis."

"Task logged."

Smiling, Luke turned his head towards Malc. "You could make a new career as a vacuum cleaner." Then, trying to tease Malc, he added, "That'd really suck."

"I assume that you are using two different definitions of the verb, suck, for humorous effect. However, you presuppose that I would find cleaning less dignified than forensic investigation. I have no concept of dignity, boredom or excitement."

Luke laughed. "No, but you know how to kill a joke. Anyway, I want you to look for fragments of tobacco leaves or ash particles."

"There are two other means of conducting the investigation. The bodies of cigarette smokers contain nicotine, which breaks down to cotinine. If the suspects have been smoking, samples taken automatically from their toilet will contain cotinine."

In the north, everyone's state of health was monitored each time they used a toilet. Samples were taken automatically from smart toilets and analyzed. If a chemical indicative of disease were found, the person would be called to a clinic immediately.

"Would that be classed as a health issue?"

"No," Malc answered. "It would be an unusual finding and an indication of illegal activities, but not a sign of ill-health, so its presence would not be highlighted by the medical centre's computer."

"Keep it in reserve. It's probably not necessary to go that far. But you said there was another way of telling."

"Smokers usually hold a cigarette between their index and middle fingers. It results in yellow staining of the skin, although it is barely visible to the human eye on conventional brown skin."

"Useful. Thanks."

"Gratitude is not necessary," said Malc.

But it struck Luke that, after Jade, Malc was his best friend. He felt grateful even though Malc was just a machine. "You've got that scan of Mollie Gazzo's identity card. Has it been altered? Is it genuine?"

"The card appears to be perfect, yet incorrect."

The advantage of having an indoor sky was that it was always completely clear. Outside, the real thing was masked by steady snowfall. "There's something else for tomorrow," Luke said. "I still want to find out more about Rowan Pearce. Interviewing any neighbours who knew him would be a good start. It hasn't been done already, has it?"

"No."

"I bet the FI thought it wasn't worth the effort because the case was wrapped up so quickly." Luke swung his legs over the edge of the bed. "So, that's a trip back to London. But right now," he said, "I've got something urgent to do. Give me a connection to Jade. I want to find out whether her gig was utterly brilliant or just great. Then I'm going to hit the sack."

"That is a curious and pointless activity."

Chapter Eight

In the morning, Luke timed his arrival at Rufus Vile and Mollie Gazzo's house to catch them as they returned from their nightshift at the power station. Watching them carefully, he saw them grimace as they caught sight of him and Malc. They were not looking forward to another interview. But they knew that they could not refuse a forensic investigator. They let him into their house in Totley Rise.

"I'm sorry to catch you straight after work," Luke said as he went with them into the unremarkable living room, "but I'm on my way to London..."

"Lucky you," Mollie muttered with irony.

Luke realized from her expression that she was trying to come across as composed, but she failed. He could see tension in her eyes and face. "Yeah. I've got to get going in a few minutes so I won't keep you for long." He let them both sink into the leather sofa before he asked, "What am I interrupting? How do you normally relax after work?"

Rufus reddened and Mollie tried to come up with something plausible. "We... er... like to share a drink and a bite to eat. That sort of thing." Weakly, she ran out of ideas straightaway and stopped talking.

Luke smiled. Even before Malc reported on the analysis he was conducting as he perched on the small table in the middle of the room, Luke was sure that the couple would normally smoke cigarettes. "You can't really call it breakfast, can you? Not after work. Anyway, have you thought about what I said, about how you got to be paired?"

"Not really. You know. We've been busy."

"Have you heard of cotinine?"

They both looked bewildered. "No."

"It's a breakdown product of nicotine and it's found in people who smoke tobacco illegally."

Taken by surprise, they both jolted, but they were not yet ready to admit anything. "What's that got to do with us?" Mollie asked, her voice quaking.

"I can tell Malc to search your house, you know. It'd be interesting to see what he turns up. Any moment now, he's going to complete an examination of the dust in here."

"All right," Rufus began. "We…"

"Roof!" Mollie warned him.

Rufus coughed into his hand. Dejected, he looked at his partner and said, "It's no use, love. You know what he wants. We've got to…"

Malc interrupted them. "There are traces of ash and tobacco in the room. In addition, staining on the forefingers of both subjects is typical of cigarette smoking."

The mobile's brief statement ended Mollie's resistance.

Luke looked at her. "How did the information on your identity card come to be wrong?"

It was Rufus who answered. "Would you really report us for smoking?"

"I can't stop Malc logging any crime with The Authorities. That's what he's programmed to do. But, if you cooperate with me, I won't pursue it. I'll tell them you were helpful to my case. That'd count in your favour."

Quietly, Mollie said, "If we say anything, what'll happen about us, our pairing?"

"I honestly don't know. Now the mistake's been made, I reckon it doesn't serve any purpose to undo it." He shrugged. "I'll do what I can because I'm on your side. *If* you help me out."

They looked at each other and came to an unspoken agreement. Mollie said, "I… er… know a woman in Derby. She was at my school. Brilliant with information technology. Even then, she could do silly things like raise an exam score by fiddling the school computer. Not that *her* grades ever needed a boost. These days, she's a programmer, working on secure systems. A real high-flier."

"So, she fiddles identity cards now?"

Mollie nodded. "She did me a favour, that's all. Just a tweak of my age. It's not a big thing."

Luke nodded in agreement. "What's her name?"

Mollie swallowed and looked down at the carpet. "Do I have to say?"

"I think you know the answer to that."

Sighing, Mollie glanced at Rufus and then asked, "You don't have to tell her it was me who gave you her name, do you?"

"I can avoid it." If it helped him to advance the case, Luke was prepared to pamper to Mollie's wishes. "I'll say Malc scanned your identity card and managed to trace it back to her."

"All right," Mollie replied reluctantly. "She's called Sadie Kershaw."

"Thank you," said Luke, getting to his feet. "I don't think I'll have to pester you any more."

As he sped south, Luke wondered what proportion of his life was spent in cabs. Of course, if he asked Malc to work it out, he'd get an exact percentage. Instead, he said, "From now on, everywhere we go for the pairing corruption case, I want you to analyse for traces of tobacco or cigarette ash. All right? Let me know if you get a whiff."

"Logged."

"Right. Back to Everton Kohter. Tell me everything you know about Rowan Pearce up to the point he was murdered."

"Files contain very little information. He went to Ealing School and graduated as an electrician at the age of seventeen. Up to his death, he had two jobs. First, he worked as an electrician for a builder, installing wiring in new properties. After losing that post, he was employed by the local authorities, maintaining electrical systems in schools and hospitals. He was not highly regarded."

"That's it?"

"Confirmed."

"What about his partner, Camilla Bunker?"

"Also an electrician, she worked in the transport industry."

"You mean, like electric cabs?"

"Correct. Her duties also involved the electrical control of auto-shipping and aeroplanes."

"Is that why she was on a plane when it crashed?"

"Confirmed."

Luke gazed at the white world beyond the window. While he watched the snow, he thought about Everton Kohter and his own chances of being paired with Jade. He didn't hold out much hope for either. He also felt guilty that he was comparing Everton's coming execution with his own pairing. One was a matter of life or death, the other was merely a kick in the teeth. But it felt worse than that to Luke. And both were permanent arrangements.

Interrupting Luke's thoughts, Malc asked, "You put the searching of health data for Mollie Gazzo and Rufus Vile on reserve. Do you wish to abandon the approach of measuring their cotinine levels?"

"Yes," Luke answered. "It doesn't matter any more. The threat of doing it was enough. Maybe, the way I put it, they thought I'd already done it."

"You use language skilfully."

Surprised, Luke turned towards his mobile. "Thanks for that opinion, Malc."

"I do not have opinions," he replied. "I was stating a fact established through observation."

Luke laughed. "Well, thanks for the fact, then." Returning the compliment, he added, "You're pretty good with facts yourself."

Luke knew that Malc would not respond. A mobile aid to law and crime did not understand praise. Even so, Luke liked to think he shared a mutual respect with Malc.

Luke hesitated outside the house that had once belonged to Rowan Pearce and Camilla Bunker. It was part of a terrace that had seen better days. Typical of a London walkway, the area was being taken over by nature. One house had an alarming crack in its brickwork. The tear was narrow at walkway level but widened until it reached the roof. It looked as if the property would fall apart before long. The next property had lost most of its tiles. Its windows were broken and the frames rotten. It appeared to have been abandoned.

Outside Rowan Pearce's house, the trees were thriving better than the buildings, apart from one dead birch. Its lifeless trunk was split almost into two as if a giant axe had cleaved it. The wind had scraped its brittle branches against the front wall and many had snapped. Underneath, the ground was littered with its broken twigs. The elm where Everton had sheltered, five metres from the front door, was laying claim to the extra space. The uneven walkway was strewn with weeds.

A man strode up to Luke with barely a glance at Malc. "What do you want, pal?"

He seemed unconcerned that Luke was a forensic investigator and his tone was aggressive. The way he pronounced *pal* made it clear that he was anything but friendly. Malc moved to Luke's left shoulder in case he needed to fire his laser in defence, yet the man wasn't carrying a weapon openly and he didn't come within touching distance of Luke.

"I'm looking into Rowan Pearce's death."

The man looked baffled. "All done and dusted. Ain't nothing here for you now."

"Did you know him?"

"Yeah. He was all right."

"What's your name?" Luke asked.

He laughed harshly. "You don't get no name out of me, pal."

"You must identify yourself," Malc said.

"No chance," he muttered.

The man was about to turn and stride away when Luke said, "Don't worry about it. I just want to know what he was like."

The neighbour shrugged. "Rowan? Bit of a layabout. Did as little as he could get away with. Good on him, I say."

"This interview cannot be entered into case notes," Malc objected. "Anonymous comments are inadmissible."

"Inadmissible, but useful," Luke replied. Turning back to the local man, he said, "Did you know the boy who got arrested?"

"No."

"How about Camilla Bunker? Rowan's partner."

"She was dead."

"Yes, but what was she like?"

"Wiry. You know? You couldn't see her if she stood sideways. Thin lips, thin neck, thin everything."

Luke nodded. "But what sort of person was she?"

"A pain. Always talking about getting out of London. Seemed to think Rowan was holding her back. He was lazy, hardly ever any credit on his identity card. She was all for getting on in life. Work, work, work and move north. Didn't suit Rowan."

"So, you'd say they clashed quite a bit?"

His deep laugh sounded as if he'd got gravel in his throat. "That's one way of putting it."

"How would you put it?"

He paused, searching for a word. "Turbulent. Like the planes she used to work on." Then he sniggered again. "I can laugh because I didn't have to live with her. Always had to have the last word, she did. Real mean and nasty.

Better for everyone she's where she is now – dead."

"Did you ever see anyone else going in or out of their house?"

"No."

"Were you around on the day he died?"

The man hesitated, clearly suspicious that Luke might accuse him of something. "You've got the lad who done it."

"Yeah, but more inside information would be good."

"All right. I was at home." He nodded towards his own house, next door. "Didn't see nothing. And no one heard nothing because of the storm."

"Was Rowan used to leaving his front door open?"

"Are you crazy? Do you want to invite bandits and muggers in? And murderers."

"Okay," Luke said. "That's all. Thanks."

Chapter Nine

Luke talked to a few more people living in the same walkway but he didn't learn any more. He'd come a long way to shed only a little light on the victim's life but he was content. The journey was worth the time it had taken because, while the gain was small, he thought that it was significant. On his way back to Sheffield, he said, "Rowan and Camilla's pairing was stormy. Like the weather."

"Irrelevant," Malc replied. "Her death occurred before his murder."

"Yes," Luke said thoughtfully. "Look, Malc. It's incredibly difficult to go into an enclosed space without leaving a trace. So, think about who went into Rowan Pearce's house. We've only got evidence for the two people who lived there, plus Everton Kohter. So, let's say the three of them were the only ones. Just as an exercise, let's assume for the moment Everton didn't do it." Before Malc could object to dismissing the obvious suspect and convict, Luke continued, "That narrows things right down. Rowan's wounds couldn't be self-inflicted, could they?"

"No."

"So, his wife – Camilla Bunker – killed him."

"Impossible. She died before the crime took place. Your error follows from an illogical assumption. Everton Kohter is guilty."

"But if he's not, logic says Camilla Bunker survived the plane crash and committed the murder. Her smeared prints were on the knife. And remember the one in the kitchen? You said it was rejected because it was marked. What if it wasn't a glitch? Maybe she had a scar on her finger."

"There is no record of such an injury in her medical files."

"My point exactly. She could've picked it up in the crash and went back to the house, knowing everyone thought she was dead. That's a pretty good alibi."

"Speculation."

"Yeah, but I owe it to Everton to check it out. Tell me about this plane crash."

Malc searched The Authorities' remote database for a few seconds before finding the air traffic accident file. "Flight GGW17 came down in Coventry after running out of fuel. Soon after take-off in London, it was struck by lightning. The aeroplane's monitor gave unusual readings from the fuel tank, indicating a rapid loss of fuel. The pilot's conversations with ground control reveal that he was convinced the readings were due to a computer malfunction caused by the lightning. He consulted an onboard electrician – presumed to be Camilla Bunker – who confirmed that an electrostatic surge could affect the computer. Afterwards, investigations confirmed that the lightning did no damage at all. Strikes on aircraft are not uncommon. As in this case, lightning usually passes harmlessly through the outer skin of the craft. In fact, the fuel line had loosened catastrophically because an engineer had fitted an incorrect nut during maintenance, causing a severe leak. The escaping aviation fuel would not have been seen by the crew or passengers because it was a night flight."

"Let me guess. The pilot didn't turn back and make an emergency landing. He carried on thinking he'd got lots of fuel – despite what his monitor said. Until he ran out."

"Confirmed. Transport crash investigators concluded that pilot error was mostly to blame. He seemed unwilling to believe that fuel could leak out at such a high rate."

"At least the plane wouldn't have caught fire. When it came down, it didn't have any fuel."

"It is correct that it had exhausted its supply, but there was an explosion and extensive fire because it crashed onto Coventry Chemical Industrial Zone. There was also spillage of several corrosive chemicals."

"That's tough. It lost its own fuel and landed on someone else's." Luke shook his head as he gazed out of the window. "We'll be going close to Coventry. I don't suppose there's much left to look at now."

"All fragments were taken away for examination in a hangar at Birmingham Airport."

"Did they find Camilla Bunker's body – or any part of it?"
"No."

"Interesting."

"There were eighteen other victims who were never found. It is thought that they were incinerated completely."

"Were there any survivors?"

"No. In aircraft accidents of this type, the chance of survival is less than five per cent."

Alert, Luke glanced at Malc. "Five per cent isn't zero, if I remember my maths."

"Correct."

To Malc, the statistics meant that Camilla Bunker was almost certainly killed. The same statistics told Luke that it was possible she had lived.

"How do plane crashes get investigated?" Luke asked.

"The procedure is similar to that at a crime scene. A transport crash investigator, or TCI, takes the place of a forensic investigator. The equivalent of a mobile aid to law and crime is a specialist unit called Masta - a Mobile Aid at Sites of Transport Accidents."

"Does a Masta take a scan of the crash site, like you'd keep a record of a crime scene?"

"Confirmed."

"So, you could request all the details and give me a hologram of the whole area?"

"That is ambitious, but possible in principle. I would require at least one Masta unit to increase processing capacity."

"Are you saying you're inferior to a Masta?" Luke asked

with a mischievous grin.

"Incorrect. I am more advanced," Malc replied without a hint of pride in his voice. "But I would need extra processors to manage the large amount of data."

"Superior, but modest," Luke said.

"I am simply stating the requirements."

"All right, Malc. Contact The Authorities. Request the data, a great big empty space, and any help you need to recreate the crash site."

"Transmitting."

"That's not all. We'll go past Derby later as well. Try to find out where Sadie Kershaw is and get me an interview with her."

"Logged."

Luke held out his card with *Luke Harding, Forensic Investigator* printed across the top and Sadie Kershaw scrutinized it closely. Then, mystified, she looked around. "Where's your mobile?"

Malc had argued about being left outside but Luke had insisted. He anticipated that Sadie would admit to nothing if Malc were on hand to record her words. "This isn't official business," he told her. "At least, not yet."

"What is it, then?"

"I'm after a new identity card."

"You've got to go through The Authorities' official procedure."

Luke shook his head. "I don't want anyone to know about it."

Sadie was in her early twenties and she was sitting in front of a computer workstation in the Registry Department of Derby's plush Town Hall. She spread out her arms in a gesture of innocence. "That's called forgery. Nothing to do with me. It's a serious crime. You'll know that."

Luke grabbed a seat, dragged it close to her and sat down. "Let me explain," he said in a hushed voice. "I've got a trail from a fake identity card back to you. For certain. If I bring my mobile in, you get into a lot of trouble. I can't stop him reporting his findings to The Authorities so it's best we sort it out here and now. Just the two of us. You see, I've got a pairing problem. The only way I can see to get around it is a change of card. I'm an FI and the girl I want to be paired with..."

Sadie interrupted. "Hold on. Even if I could do something like that, what does *she* think of all this?"

"Jade agrees. But altering her card to make her look like a scientist won't wash with the committee because she's well known as a musician. And getting more well known by the day. Altering mine is even less likely to work. My job's too high profile. The only idea that stands a chance is giving us both new and false identities. Then we go somewhere we're not known, except through our new identity cards. Compatible identity cards." Luke was aiming to tempt a forger into the open. That's all. He was laying another trap. The idea was far too fanciful to put into practice. He couldn't give up his role of investigator any more than Jade could tear herself away from music.

Sadie glanced around and then leaned towards him. She whispered, "It's true I've helped out a few women. Ones I felt sorry for. Ones who come up against stupid rules, stopping them achieving what they want."

Luke nodded. "What have I got to do?"

"Let me speak to Jade. Not through a telescreen. That can be monitored. Bring her to me, face-to-face."

Luke stood up with a grateful smile on his face. "It's a deal. We'll be in touch."

Jade's appearance in front of Sheffield Pairing Committee took only a few seconds.

Ms Boniwell asked her, "Are you content with your pairing arrangement?"

"No."

"Is it true that you'd prefer to be paired with Forensic Investigator Luke Harding?"

"Yes."

"Think carefully before you answer, Jade Vernon. Would you be willing to change your career – to prove yourself in science – as a means of legalizing a pairing with him?"

For a moment, Jade closed her eyes. She didn't need long. She lifted up her head boldly and stared at the Chairperson. "No. It's the system that needs changing. Not me."

And that was it. Jade was dismissed.

Chapter Ten

The Authorities had agreed to let Luke use the original crash site to reconstruct the accident. They had already delivered three Masta units to the industrial zone in Coventry by the time that Luke and Malc arrived. The cab tracks ran right into the heart of the industrial zone for the benefit of the workers. Since the accident, though, the whole place had been shut down. The chemical industry was building a new development to the west of the Midlands because starting afresh was considered easier and cheaper than repairing this scarred estate. The area remained exactly as it was after the spilled chemicals had been washed away, the remains of the dead taken to the pathology laboratory, and the remnants of the aeroplane removed for the accident inquiry.

It looked like a rusting metal jungle, full of twisted girders, warped and crumpled towers, shattered empty warehouses, and burnt-out laboratories. It was a creepy ghost town but it reminded Luke most of a giant body with its flesh burnt away, leaving only a blackened skeleton. Where there had once been workers, vehicles, steaming chimneys, and the hefty thumps and clangs of machinery, there was now only sinister stillness.

A breeze swept through the lifeless estate but the clear cold weather was helpful to Luke and Malc. Fog, snow or rain would have interfered with the complicated projection, making the image unstable and blurred.

Positioned at the corners of the triangular crash scene, the three Mastas informed Malc that they were ready to recreate the scene as a hologram. They were ready to put all of the fragments of Flight GGW17 back into place, including what remained of the plane's passengers and crew.

Talking to Luke, Malc said, "I can coordinate the reproduction when you wish."

"Off you go, then."

"Where do you wish me to go?"

Luke sighed. "I want you and your Mastas to show me a virtual reality version of the accident. I know it happened at night but give me a daylight version so I can see everything."

"Processing."

Within seconds, misshapen parts belonging to the wreck began to appear as if they were growing rapidly out of the ground. The battered tailfin, detached from the rest of the fuselage, appeared on top of a two-storey building. Below it, the rear part of the main body expanded like an inflating balloon until it was the correct size. The smashed nose cone materialized like the cracked shell of a colossal egg against a distillation tower. From where Luke stood, he could see right into the pilot's cabin. He could still recognize seats and a bank of controls.

In between the nose and the tail, the main part of the fuselage lay, diced into three sections. One of them had swivelled so that it was at right angles to the other two. Another had rolled onto its side. One wing was nowhere to be seen. It must have been thrown behind one of the buildings or exploded into hundreds of pieces. The other was a mangled mess but it still hung on grimly to the rest of the aeroplane. It formed a bridge from the fractured fuselage to the wood at the edge of the estate.

Cargo was scattered all around Luke. Surveying the chaos, he could make out parts of suitcases and packages but most of the wreckage was too badly burnt or splintered or corroded to be identifiable. There were a few bits of charred paper, a couple of identity cards, and scraps of clothing as well. In reality, all of these morsels had long since been collected by TCIs and taken away for identification. Each had become a small piece in a giant three-dimensional jigsaw puzzle when investigators had built a complete picture of the disaster. The larger pieces, like the intact wing and chunks of the main body, had been airlifted to Birmingham Airport. Malc had downloaded all of the findings so that he could identify most of the unrecognisable remains.

Luke let out a long breath. The nightmare that had suddenly sprung up in front of his eyes was disheartening. He couldn't imagine the terror of being involved in such devastation and, as an FI, he didn't know where to start his own investigation.

"You said they didn't find Camilla Bunker."

"Confirmed."

"Was anything of hers found?"

"Yes. Her pairing ring – inscribed with her partner's initials and her own – and her identity card. The card was damaged by fire and acid spilling from a ruptured storage tank, but it was partly readable."

"Where was it found?"

"I will show you."

Luke followed Malc as his mobile glided above the relics of the accident. Luke was tempted to be careful where he put his feet, imagining that he was treading on valuable evidence. But he didn't. He told himself that it was okay to stride carelessly through it because it wasn't real.

It seemed odd to Luke that there was no smell. The air should have been foul, almost unbearable with the stench of burning, death and a cocktail of chemicals. But the noxious fumes would have blown away years ago.

The likeness of Camilla Bunker's identity card, part clear, part scorched, was lying on an ordinary concrete corridor in the V-shape formed by the middle section of fuselage and the buckled wing. The likeness of Camilla's face on the plastic surface had blackened beyond recognition and the edge of the card was touching an evil-looking pool of liquid.

Luke squatted down and narrowed his eyes. "Is this water?"

"No. It was sulphuric acid from the chemical works."

"What would happen if someone walked through all this?"

Malc answered, "It depends on the material, quality and thickness of the shoes, but acid of this concentration would have corroded them quickly. However, you should remember that the greater danger would have been the intense fire."

"Mmm." Luke was about to stand up when a black lump a metre to his left caught his eye. It was thicker at one end than the other, like a burnt log. He pointed to it and asked, "What's that?"

"It was a human foot."

Luke recoiled and swallowed. "Not Camilla's."

"The intense heat degraded any DNA so identification was not possible."

Beyond it was a small collection of stumps like burnt chips. "Are they what I think they are?" Luke said with a frown.

"I do not know what you are thinking. They are unidentified fingers."

Luke nodded and shuddered. "This place gives me the creeps. How many died, Malc?"

"Seventy-seven."

Sometimes, Luke wished he were like Malc: completely immune to horror. Then he wouldn't feel the need to weep. To keep back the tears, he stood up and said,

"Where was she? Camilla. Which seat?"

"She travelled in Row 15. That was in the middle segment."

Luke glanced at the wrecked, hollow tube, punctuated with a line of broken windows. The outer shell of the fuselage was folded back like the opened lid of a can of food.

"You cannot go into it because it is not really there. However, I can strip it away layer by layer to show you the inside."

"Let me see her seat, please."

The skin of the aeroplane dissolved, revealing a cross-section of the metallic body. Malc adjusted the hologram so that Row 15 glowed red. There were three deformed seats. Two were empty. The third was occupied by a skeleton in what appeared to be ripped black clothing. It was probably charred skin.

Luke shook his head in despair. "Enough. Where did they find her pairing ring?"

"On the ground at the back of this section. It would have been Row 31 if the fuselage had remained intact."

At once, Luke frowned. "Well away from her identity card. How come it ended up back there?"

"The speculation at the time was that, after the flesh burned away, the ring rolled..."

"Look at the angle, Malc. The plane nose-dived. If it rolled anywhere, it would've ended up at the front, near Row 1."

"That's why there were alternative possible explanations. She could have been in conversation with someone near Row 31 at the time of the accident, or she might have been exercising her legs, or returning from the toilet, situated at the rear of the craft."

Luke shook his head in disbelief. "At the first sign of trouble, surely the crew would've told her to go back to her seat if she wasn't in it."

"Likely, but not known."

Luke took a deep breath of the curiously fresh air. "What's over there, where I can't see?" He pointed beyond the broken aeroplane.

"The canal. It was used to ship products from the factories to warehouses and suppliers."

Luke turned and walked parallel with the discoloured wing, towards the muddy verge where the industrial zone gave way to a wood. His foot went through the virtual version of a warped emergency door that had flown off the main body of the plane. He stopped when he saw what was lying next to it. "Give me a hand here, Malc."

"Impossible. I do not have..."

"I mean, tell me where this came from." He pointed to a plastic bottle full of water. "Did a TCI leave it here or was it from an engineer working on the site?"

"No. It came from the aeroplane."

"What?" Luke exclaimed. "Look! The place is like a bombsite. How could it have survived?"

"Some items were blown clear, did not catch fire, or were protected from damage in some way by their surroundings. It may appear odd but it is normal at crash sites. A few artefacts are frequently recovered intact."

Luke wagged a finger at Malc. "If a bottle of water can survive in one piece, why not a person as well? Why not Camilla Bunker? Maybe she was thrown clear, didn't go up in flames, or was protected somehow."

Malc hesitated for an instant. Then he said, "That is valid reasoning."

Chapter Eleven

The tip of the lame wing rested on the wet soil at the boundary of the wood. Luke wandered around it, looking carefully at the ground. Then he asked, "Was this scan taken before investigators walked all over the place?"

"Confirmed."

"What did they make of these footprints, then?"

Malc searched the file notes. "There is no entry describing impressions of shoes at this location. I conclude that they were not regarded as significant."

The illusion of the soft ground on the day of the accident was lying over the present-day scene like a carpet. Bizarrely, Luke's shoes sank through it as he stood on the real earth below and examined patterns in the soil that the weather had long since eroded.

The first print had been made by a left shoe with its heel towards the wing and its toe pointing away, towards the wood. A stride away, there was the matching impression of a right shoe. There were two more prints before the hologram reached its outer limit. Something else intrigued Luke. There was a set of the same shoeprints returning to the site. He could not tell where the trail led because the soil gave way to the concrete corridor – a hard surface that left no impressions. The third and final shoe impressions led back into the wood, paralleling the first ones he'd noticed.

Luke looked back towards the shattered aeroplane and said, "Someone could have walked out of the fuselage – where the emergency exit used to be or just through one of the holes – and onto the wing." He pointed to the spot. "It's not far from Row 15. From up there, maybe Camilla could see the ground was covered in chemicals by the light of the fire. She could have used the wing as a bridge over it all."

"It would have been very hot."

"Okay. She ran along the wing and jumped down here. She headed for the wood but then stopped and came back. Why would anyone come back when it'd be dangerous? Flames everywhere. Acid and other stuff. Explosions, maybe."

Malc said, "This is gross speculation but, if there were a survivor who returned, the likely purpose would be to salvage something."

"Mmm." Luke shook his head. "What about the opposite? Maybe she wanted to leave something behind."

He took out his own slender identity card and, taking careful aim, he skimmed it towards the vision of the crashed plane. It cut through the air and flew several metres beyond the spot where he'd seen the remains of Camilla Bunker's identity card. He raced after the valuable rectangle of plastic and retrieved it from under the holographic layer.

Luke thought about his idea some more. "Okay, Malc. Pure theory. Nothing more than that. But bear with me. Somehow, like the bottle of water, Camilla Bunker survived the impact. She clambered out of a crack in the plane and saw the place on fire and awash with chemicals. Dreadful smell. Her first reaction was to run. She dashed over the wing." His eyes followed her imagined path as he walked back to the spot where he'd seen the footprints. "In a daze, maybe, she wandered into the wood. But then her brain clicked into gear. She saw a real opportunity. She could get away with all sorts if everyone thought she was dead. She came back and, to convince us she died, threw her identity card into the mess from somewhere around here. I've just proved it's possible to skim it to where it was. Then, to make sure, she also chucked her pairing ring – because it was marked with her initials. Malc, find me a stone about the same weight as her ring."

His mobile dissolved the holographic image near the wing tip. At the edge of the corridor, there was a small piece of broken concrete. His laser highlighted it.

Luke reached down and grabbed it. Standing upright again, he threw it towards the back section of the fuselage. It landed close to the spot where the investigators had found Camilla Bunker's pairing ring. "There. Bob's your uncle. It's possible to chuck both things from here, without going into the flames. Thinking she'd left enough behind to convince everyone she'd burnt to a cinder, she went back into the wood. It gave her good cover while she sneaked away – maybe with an injury to her finger."

"None of this is invalid reasoning," Malc announced, "but all of the evidence in its favour is too ambiguous to be entered into case notes."

Luke pointed downwards. "Shoeprints, Malc. I want you to try and check them against Camilla Bunker's size. Anyway, they tell us one passenger came here twice."

"That is likely, but not proven," Malc replied. "Two people in similar shoes could have come once each."

Luke laughed. "Come off it! Next, you'll claim someone with one leg could've hopped here four times."

"That is incorrect. The impressions clearly show both left and right shoes."

Luke threw up his arms. "It was a joke. And don't even start on the possibility that someone was walking backwards. Let's look for real evidence. I reckon she escaped across the wing. She was probably bleeding from her finger, maybe with other injuries. Was there any blood on the top of this wing? Or anything else significant?"

"Unknown. Any chemical evidence was completely degraded by heat."

"How about hospitals? Check if any medical centres in the area treated a woman who could've been Camilla Bunker but who couldn't produce an identity card. As well as the finger, she might've had fire or acid burns.

Maybe more."

"Task logged. I will complete the electronic inquiries as soon as possible." Malc paused before adding, "You should know that there were traces of illegally imported cigarettes in the hold."

"Really? Interesting. Or pure coincidence."

"Insufficient data. No conclusions were reached by the inquiry team, other than the fact that someone had smuggled tobacco on board."

Luke took a last look at the crash site and then said, "I don't think I'm going to squeeze any more out of this, Malc. You can shut it down."

The wreckage proved that it was no more than a mirage by disappearing as quickly as a picture fading from a telescreen when the power was turned off. Here, though, Luke was left with much more than a blank screen. It reverted to a ruined industrial zone that reminded him of London.

In the cab, Luke thought about Camilla Bunker. If he was right, she had been caught up in the accident unwittingly, survived it, and taken advantage of the circumstances. Or maybe his imagination was in overdrive. Maybe he was turning a simple situation — Camilla killed in a plane crash, Rowan killed by Everton Kohter — into an unlikely tangle. Why would his brain do that? Because he was naturally suspicious and naturally sympathetic towards Everton.

Interrupting Luke's thoughts, Malc reported, "I have received replies to my inquiries about medical admissions near the crash site. There were no known living patients. No one presented themselves with injuries consistent with the crash and no one tried to get treatment without an identity card within five days of the accident."

Luke nodded slowly. "Thanks. I suppose it makes sense. If Camilla was trying to play dead, she's not going to turn up at a hospital. Maybe she just gashed her finger and that's no big deal."

"I have also searched all known files to discover her shoe size. No such record remains." Malc did not sound disappointed. To him, it was simply another result to be reported to a forensic investigator and logged. He always announced success and failure with the same bland tone.

Luke was not immune to disappointment. He allowed himself a groan but he wouldn't let it get him down while he had other leads. "Were there any muddy shoeprints in Rowan Pearce's house that didn't match Everton's?"

"No."

Luke muttered to himself, "Either she wasn't there or she was careful."

"Correct," Malc replied as if Luke had been talking to him.

"Can you get a picture of her?"

"There are no images of her on file."

"Not even in Rowan's case notes?"

"No. She was neither a suspect nor a witness. Her earlier death made her irrelevant to the investigation."

"Where do I go from here?" Luke asked himself.

"You requested to return to Sheffield."

"Yes," Luke said, closing his eyes and smiling at Malc's misunderstanding. "To Jade's place and then to Derby."

"Is Jade Vernon relevant to your investigation?"

"She is now, yes. You see, Sadie Kershaw wanted to speak to her about identity cards. I'm very eager to speak to Sadie about the same thing."

"Explain."

"It's obvious. Camilla Bunker left her identity card in Coventry. If she survived, she could live rough without one, but that wouldn't be good enough for a woman like her. She was ambitious. That's why she killed Rowan. If she did, I mean. Anyway, she'd need an identity card to start again, to get herself a new life in the north. She'd need someone like Sadie Kershaw."

Chapter Twelve

Leaving Luke and Malc in a restaurant near the centre of Derby, Jade went to Sadie Kershaw's third-floor apartment alone. The two of them hit it off almost straightaway, especially when Sadie confessed that she'd heard quite a few of Jade's pieces and downloaded several so that she could listen again. Jade was always delighted when she came across someone who enjoyed her music. Now, she felt thrilled and uncomfortable at the same time. She was visiting Sadie at Luke's request to play the part of an aggrieved girlfriend wanting a new identity card. Or was her role an assistant forensic investigator? Either way, she wasn't there as herself — as a musician or a friend — so she felt like a cheat.

It didn't take long for Sadie to hint that she could make Jade a new identity card but she added, "I don't know how it's going to help you, though."

"How do you mean?" Jade asked.

Sadie laughed. "Come off it. You're not going to give up music for anyone, are you? You love it. In a way, you're already paired with music, not a man."

Jade couldn't stand the deception any more. She became herself again. "Look, you're being really nice to me and I'm being..."

"A forensic investigator's spy?"

"Something like that," Jade admitted, wishing she'd never agreed to go along with Luke's scheme.

"The thing is, he's just doing his job," Sadie said. "I know he's after me, but there was something desperate and genuine in his eyes. He'd go a long way to pair with you. That's kind of romantic."

"He'd go a long way to clinch a case as well," she replied. "Once he gets his teeth into something, he doesn't let go."

"I guessed that."

"But you're still falling into his trap."

Sadie shrugged as if she didn't have a care in the world. "He's already got evidence against me, but he hasn't arrested me. I don't think it's me he's after. Not really."

In the restaurant, Luke sipped his fruit juice and then glanced in turn at his two companions. One was warm, human and never failed to make him feel good. The other was a cold metal box that never failed to provide him with assistance. Both were loyal to him but neither would hesitate to criticize him in their different ways when he was making a mistake or being too reckless.

Luke put his drink down on the table and spoke quietly. "I still don't understand why the Pairing Committee went ahead and matched Mollie Gazzo with Rufus Vile if one of the members got Mollie's real age from files. Either that person was bribed in some way to tell the committee her identity card was right, or it's all a big hoax and I'm being set up. If there's something going on between The Authorities and the Pairing Committee designed to test me, Mollie and Rufus are just actors in the game plan. The question is, where does that leave Sadie Kershaw? Is she another actor, or are The Authorities out to get her as well?"

Jade interrupted. "She's on the level, I'm sure. Not acting."

"Maybe The Authorities know what she's been doing and they're after her as well as me. They might be killing two birds with one stone."

At once, Malc replied, "I am not aware of an avian connection. While the killing of common birds is not a crime, endangered species are..."

Despite the seriousness of the situation, Jade giggled.

Luke said, "Never mind, Malc. There's something far more important in this. If The Authorities used Mollie to ask Sadie to forge her an identity card..." He fell silent as he thought about the implications.

Malc said what was on Luke's mind. "It would be against the law." In Malc's programming, truth, the law and logic came above everything else. He continued, "Incitement to commit a crime is itself a crime."

"Exactly," Luke replied. "The Authorities might've broken the law. I hope so, anyway."

"Hope so?" Jade queried.

"If they can bend the rules for their own ends, they can

bend them for us." He finished his juice and said, "Are we ready, then?"

Jade gulped down the last of her drink as well. "As ready as I'll ever be."

"What about you, Malc?"

"I am always ready as long as there is power in my batteries."

"Yes, but I want you to record this interview and keep it to yourself. I don't want you to pass it to The Authorities."

"I cannot comply because it is against my instructions."

"But who are we investigating?"

"Sadie Kershaw. A programmer of secure systems."

"Yes," Luke replied. "As well as Sheffield Pairing Committee, Mollie Gazzo and Rufus Vile. You wouldn't send them details of the case against them, would you?"

"No."

"But you've just agreed The Authorities might be guilty of inciting a crime. I'm obliged to investigate, aren't I?"

"Correct."

"Well, you can't send case notes to the suspects. It doesn't make sense."

Malc hesitated for several seconds. "I am not programmed for such circumstances."

"All right," Luke said. "What's your first duty?"

"Upholding the law."

"You can do that best by keeping information to yourself until we figure out what's going on. Agreed?"

Malc took an extra two seconds to reach a conclusion. "Logic requires me to withhold information that might implicate The Authorities in a criminal activity."

"Right," Luke replied with a grin. "Now we're ready. Let's get going."

Sadie's quarters were at the rear of the apartment block. Behind her, there was a balcony with a view over Derwent Park and the river. Sadie herself was wearing a puzzled expression as she glanced from Jade to Malc and finally fixed her eyes on Luke. "I'm getting a mixed message here," she said to him. "A mobile aid to law and crime tells me everything's turned official all of a sudden. But Jade's here, so..."

Jade smiled at her with sympathy.

"Malc," Luke said, "Are you going to transmit details of this interview to The Authorities?"

"No."

Sadie was astonished. "I know these machines always tell the truth," she said, "but last time, you didn't bring it in because you said you couldn't stop it reporting its findings."

"The case has changed a bit," Luke replied, without offering a real explanation. "Do you really fake identity cards or have The Authorities told you to pretend to be a forger?"

Taken aback by the bluntness of his question, Sadie frowned. "What?"

Luke didn't need an answer. Her bewildered expression was enough to tell him that she wasn't an agent for The Authorities. "Have you heard of Mollie Gazzo?"

"Mollie? Yes. I was at school with her."

"Did you tinker with her identity card?"

Sadie hesitated.

"She tells me you changed her age by four years."

"Sounds like she's trying to get me into trouble."

Luke sat down to signal that he was prepared for a long interview. "I know you've made illegal identity cards. You offered to do it for Jade and, last time, you told me you'd helped out a few women you felt sorry for."

She sighed and whispered, "Yes. You said you'd traced one back to me."

"So, you might as well tell me about Mollie Gazzo," he replied. "In fact, there's a real possibility Mollie was acting on behalf of The Authorities when she asked you to fake her age. That means they're on to you. They could pick you up anytime, so your best bet is to cooperate with me."

While Sadie listened to him, her expression changed from confusion to alarm. "Why's that?"

"If I'm right, they've led me here – via Mollie – because they're testing if I'll put the law above my own interests. We've both been set up."

She glanced at Jade as if for reassurance.

Jade nodded. "Either Mollie's genuine and the Pairing Committee's corrupt, or it's a put-up job with you at one end and Luke at the other."

"Either way," Luke added, "you're in trouble so it'd be a good idea to keep me on your side."

"Why would Mollie agree to it, if it's all a game? What does she get out of it?"

"A supply of cigarettes from The Authorities and immunity from prosecution for smoking them, maybe," Luke answered. "And certainly the man she wanted. She might've agreed to anything for that."

"So," the programmer asked, "what are you going to do about it?"

"I'll carry on playing the game – if that's what it is – till I find out for sure – without getting you into trouble."

Sadie smiled wryly. "You can't really protect me, can you?"

"If it's all been set up to test you and me, I might be able to. If it's a genuine corruption case…" He shrugged. "That's trickier. But, if you help me with something else… Maybe."

"What's that?" Sadie prompted.

"These women you felt sorry for and helped out," Luke said, "Did they include someone called Camilla Bunker?"

Sadie didn't reply at once. She thought about it before answering. "No."

"It would've been two years ago. A twenty-six year old woman from London."

Sadie shook her head.

"Let me tell you something else I think's happened," said

Luke. "Then you won't feel so sorry for Camilla if she was one of your customers." He went through the plane crash, Rowan Pearce's murder, and Everton Kohter's terrible plight. "There's a real possibility she faked her own death to give herself a great alibi. Then she got rid of a lazy partner who was holding her back. You might have sympathy with someone wanting a fresh start and a new identity, but I bet you wouldn't be so sympathetic if you knew she'd killed her husband." He gazed into her face before adding, "If you helped her, you're partly responsible for the execution of an innocent fifteen-year-old boy."

"You go in for a lot of ifs, buts and maybes."

Luke nodded. "I'm asking you to help me clear them up. One thing's for sure. Everton will face the death penalty on Sunday the twelfth of February. Punishment doesn't get more certain – and irreversible – than that."

Sadie broke eye contact and looked nervously down at the carpet. "I don't keep records – for obvious reasons – but, no, I don't think she came to me."

Luke was still not convinced. "I just need her new name. That's all."

"Even if I'd... After all this time, I might not remember the name she'd ask for. And she might not have told me her real name anyway."

"I can't describe her much, but she was thin. Very thin and wiry."

"It doesn't mean anything to me."

"All right. Is there anybody else in the game of forging identity cards?"

Sadie reddened. Plainly, she didn't want to get anyone else into trouble. "I can't say."

Jade knelt by Sadie's seat and put both hands on her arm. "It's important. I think you should say if you know anything."

Again, Sadie shook her head.

"All right," Luke said, getting to his feet. "I'm going to get Malc to show you a picture of Everton Kohter when he was arrested. Thirteen years old. Malc, download it into Sadie's computer so she can see who we're going to execute in two weeks' time." He turned back to Sadie. "Have a good look after we've gone and think about it. Maybe then you'll remember something about Camilla Bunker or think of someone who might've given her a new identity, because that someone's condemning Everton to death. You'd better let on while there's still time." He pointed to the image of a young and scruffy Everton, looking utterly bewildered, drenched, bloodstained, with messy hair. "What do you see, Sadie? Vicious killer or confused lad? Contact me – soon. You don't want this on your conscience."

Chapter Thirteen

On Monday morning, three drops of deep red liquid spurted out of Luke's mouth and landed on the white tiles opposite him. Once he'd swallowed, Luke pointed to the small stains on the hotel wall. "From the spatter pattern, I'd say these Middle Eastern pomegranates are pretty tasty."

"The spatter pattern does not..."

"It's breakfast, Malc. A time for drinking, eating a pomegranate and cracking the occasional joke." With his little finger nail, he flicked a seed out from between two of his teeth and then concentrated on the crucial job in hand.

After breakfast and a shower, Luke always felt refreshed and ready. His brain would fill with more ideas than there were hours in the day to pursue them. "It's amazing," he said, combing his long wet hair. "I didn't think there was any link between the corruption case and Everton's, but maybe there are a couple. It looks like they're both about the forging of an identity card. And, up to now, my job's always been to prove someone's guilty of something. With these two cases, I'm trying to prove someone's innocent." He put the comb down and was about to say something else when Malc interrupted.

"I have received a transmission from Nicoletta Boniwell, requesting your presence as soon as possible."

"At the City Hall?"

"No. It is not a formal meeting. She has given me her home address."

Luke's brow creased. "All right, but, before I go, get me the medical records of the members of the Sheffield Pairing Committee."

"I can search data for members of the public but I do not have immediate access to private information on The Authorities or their committee members. I must request their permission first."

"If you ask, will The Authorities, Nicoletta and the rest know I'm checking on them?"

"Confirmed."

"Forget it then."

"I cannot forget, but I will delete the task."

"I still don't want the Pairing Committee to know I'm onto them, so I'm going to do it on the quiet." Even though he knew that Malc would respond with an immediate rebuke, Luke added, "I'll have a go at hacking into the health centre instead."

A mobile could not adopt a disapproving tone like an instructor. He said simply, "That is against the law."

"But it's a logical way forwards when I can't afford to let the suspects know what I'm doing. Anyway, if they've used underhand tactics on me, I can fight back with a bit of trickery."

"That is incorrect. There is no excuse for breaking the

law. Also, you do not have sufficient data to prove that The Authorities have acted illegally."

"That's why I need those files."

"What is your aim?"

"Anyone could bribe me with a box of pomegranates," he replied, smiling to indicate that it wasn't actually true. "If there's a cigarette smoker on the Pairing Committee, that might explain a thing or two. If it's a genuine corruption case, Mollie Gazzo might've persuaded them to ignore her real age in return for a load of tobacco. But if this whole thing's been set up by The Authorities to test me, Mollie wouldn't have had to do any bribing. No need for secret smokers and corruption on the committee. They'd just do what they're told by The Authorities — and pretend to be open to bribes." Luke sat down in front of his computer terminal. "So, I want to see if anyone on the Pairing Committee is full of cotinine. I just need to see the results from their smart toilets."

"I cannot participate in an illegal activity."

"You'd better look the other way, then. But, before you do, just give me the panel's names, apart from Nicoletta Boniwell." With a cheeky grin, he added, "Knowing their names isn't illegal."

Using his FI's identity card, Luke logged on to Sheffield Medical Centre's computer. Most software was written with security systems that could be bypassed by a mobile aid to law and crime or when presented with a forensic investigator's identity card. That way, he found some low-level passwords used to run the network. They were predictable, like *admin*, *password* and *medic*. Once he got a foot in the door, he needed to force it open wider and wider until he got into restricted medical files.

He was a little out of practice. He hadn't hacked into a confidential system since schooldays. Yet he still had a knack for it. His method was based on the fact that all computers were designed to answer questions. That was their function so their programming compelled them to do it. He probed this one with questions and sniffed the responses coming out of it. Each little packet of information gave him a better understanding of the way it worked. Patiently, he built up a picture of the operating system. Then he fished around for its high-level password policy, like the length of its secret codes and where they were stored.

Every time he gained access to another area, he delved deeper, relentlessly and patiently going up the ranking until he captured a medical administrator's password. Then it was easy to get into patients' files. For each member of the Pairing Committee, he found a list of substances found in their last few samples. Scanning laboriously and carefully down each record, he did not find a single reference to cotinine.

Straightaway, he logged off and turned to Malc. "No tobacco addicts on the Pairing Committee."

"I cannot add that information to case notes because it was obtained by illegal means."

"It doesn't prove anything for sure, either." Luke flashed a smile and added, "But it's interesting to know."

"Nicoletta Boniwell has sent a reminder of her invitation," Malc informed him.

Luke nodded. As he went for his coat, he said over his shoulder, "She's getting impatient. Good. I'm ready for her now."

Nicoletta had a plush apartment overlooking Southern Park. But it wasn't the view or the furnishing that caught Luke's eye first. It wasn't even the Chair of Sheffield Pairing Committee herself. It was the large hairy spider that covered her entire right palm that grabbed Luke's attention. He let out a small gasp.

Nicoletta smirked. "You aren't scared, are you?" Her tone wasn't very friendly. It was intended to tease.

"Not if you aren't."

"You can hold him, if you like." She held out her right hand. In comparison with the jet-black spider, the skin of her protruding fingers looked paler than normal. Her forefinger was slightly discoloured.

"No, thanks," Luke replied. "I'm pretty big from its point of view. I might scare it."

She laughed. "That's possible. He's a European wolf spider. Most people call him a tarantula."

"Isn't it poisonous?" Luke asked.

"All spiders are poisonous to some degree. They subdue and kill their prey by injecting poison, then they suck the juices out. But their fangs can't usually penetrate human skin. This one *can* bite right through but its poison is nothing to worry about. The only risk in handling him is a bit of irritation from his hairs, that's all." She stood up and walked over to a large glass tank, took off its lid and coaxed the spider back into its artificial surroundings. It crawled sluggishly onto the dry earth as if unwilling to leave her warm hand. "It's a pity spiders have got such a bad reputation because most aren't dangerous to us at all. When people say they're scared, it's all in the mind."

She returned to her seat and waved Luke towards another chair. Uninvited, Malc settled on a sideboard. Nicoletta glanced at the mobile but talked only to Luke. "Your... friend, Jade Vernon, would know all about a folk dance from southern Europe. It's got a fascinating history. Once, people thought they'd suffer fatal depression if a tarantula bit them. The only cure was to dance like crazy until the symptoms had gone." She shook her head and smiled. "The dance was infectious. All very jolly to cancel out the depression. Everyone joined in. A type of mass hysteria took over whole villages. Eventually, someone put the dance to music and it was called the tarantella — after the spider."

"I didn't know," Luke admitted. "But I thought we'd get

around to Jade one way or another."

"Yes. You must know why you're here." She raised her left hand, flashing her pairing ring with its sizeable sapphire.

Luke nodded. He realized he was about to hear the Pairing Committee's verdict, but there was more to the visit than that. Nicoletta could have announced the outcome by telescreen or called him to a formal meeting in the City Hall. He knew she'd invited him to her apartment for a different reason and he had already guessed what it was.

She said, "Last week, I told you not to hold out much hope. I have some sympathy with your claim personally, but the committee wasn't impressed with your argument for pairing with Ms Vernon. They seemed to think you were trying to pull rank as a forensic investigator, trying to get special treatment. I'm sorry."

Luke looked away. "Well, you did warn me, but I'm still…"

"Disappointed. I can tell." She paused before adding, "I suppose I could raise the issue with my colleagues again because it's not a *final* decision. But you'd have to give me more to work with, if you see what I mean."

In the far corner, one of Nicoletta's pets was crawling up the glass wall of its enclosure. It was unusual to see a spider from the underside and it looked less creepy that way. Next to the glass cage, there was an air freshening unit.

"You don't have to figure anything out now," she

continued. "Go away and have a think about it. If you don't contact me, I'll ratify your pairing with Georgia Bowie. If you do, I'll see if I can change anything. But," she said, standing up, "you must understand the odds are still stacked against you."

Luke was not surprised by the decision. More than that, it was exactly what he'd expected, so he wasn't shocked. Adopting a tone midway between sadness and defiance, he replied, "All right. I'll be in touch. Definitely."

Chapter Fourteen

As soon as the door slid shut behind Luke and he stepped out into the cold walkway, he turned towards Malc. "I bet you've got something to tell me."

"Are you referring to my analysis of the apartment?"

With a grin, Luke mimicked his mobile. "Confirmed." He was now so sure that he was witnessing The Authorities laying a trap for him that he could predict Malc's findings. He was convinced that Nicoletta Boniwell was mimicking a cigarette smoker.

"The air contained traces of tobacco smoke and the dust on the surface of the sideboard included cigarette ash."

Luke nodded. "She'd got some yellow on her forefinger as well." He laughed quietly to himself. "She went out of her way with some dye, I guess, to make sure it was noticeable."

Obstinate, Malc noted, "The evidence indicates that she smokes tobacco."

"But she doesn't," Luke replied. "There wasn't any cotinine in her metabolic profile."

"Inadmissible."

"She's laying a false trail, wanting me to think she's hooked on cigarettes," Luke claimed. "Why did she ask me to her apartment? To give you the opportunity to detect tobacco. She's planted the evidence, Malc. She even had the spider in her hand for a reason. She used it to draw attention to the yellow patch on her finger."

"Without valid data to the contrary, you have sufficient evidence to charge Nicoletta Boniwell with cigarette smoking."

"That's what you're supposed to think. Get your electrons round this, Malc. I'm supposed to deduce that she took a tobacco bribe from Mollie Gazzo and Rufus Vile. It's The Authorities' way of inviting me to find a source of cigarettes and bribe her with them. She said, 'I could raise the subject again, but you'd have to give me more to work with, if you see what I mean.' If you see what I mean! *You* don't see what she means because you don't understand people. But I do. It was a prompt to buy her off. And if I tried – to pair with Jade – I'd be in deep trouble, probably out of a career."

"In law, that is speculation."

"Could someone smoke tobacco and not have cotinine in their metabolic profile?"

"It would take several days for cotinine to pass out of the human body following consumption of a cigarette. Regular smokers would always have it in their profiles."

"It's all a con, then. And I can prove it. We're going back in and you're going to get close enough to scan the colour on her right forefinger without her knowing. Can you do that?"

"What information are you hoping to gain?"

"Is it a dye or a real smoker's stain?"

"I may already have sufficient data to distinguish these possibilities by comparing the yellow tint of Nicoletta Boniwell's forefinger with that of the two known smokers in normal light. Infrared spectroscopic examination may not be necessary."

"Okay. Do it now."

Luke rocked back and forth on his feet, switching his weight alternately from his heel to his toes in an attempt to keep them warm.

After a minute, Malc said, "The wavelength of the staining on Nicoletta Boniwell's right forefinger is different from that of Mollie Gazzo and Rufus Vile. According to my library of visible spectra, the absorption of light corresponds exactly to turmeric."

"Turmeric?"

"It is the natural yellow dye used to colour curries."

"Why would she rub curry powder on her finger, Malc?"

"It would appear to be an attempt to deceive you into thinking that she smokes cigarettes."

Luke beamed. "That *can* go into case notes."

"Already logged."

Luke did not allow himself long to celebrate. "It's true, then. This is my big test. I'm supposed to conclude she smokes and charge her with an illegal act and arrest her on suspicion of corruption. Or I take advantage of the situation and bribe her to pair me with Jade. The Authorities will be waiting and watching to see which way I jump, to see if I pass or fail their loyalty test." Heading back towards the freeway, he added, "The FI in me wants one thing. Me – myself – I want the other. For the moment, though, I'm going to let them stew. And… Well, they're playing games with me, so I'll play games with them."

"Explain."

"You'll see. When I'm ready." He stopped walking and turned towards his mobile. "Just tell me. Are you still holding facts back from The Authorities?"

"Confirmed."

Luke smiled. He was relaxed now because he felt in control and he could see a way forwards. "Good. Keep it like that or I'm snookered." As soon as he said it, he put up his palm. "And don't lecture me about the value of swerve shots."

"I'm going to put more pressure on Sadie Kershaw, Malc. I want you to send her a little reminder." Luke scratched his head, thinking. "I know. Make it short and simple. Just put *Twelve days before Everton Kohter's execution* on her telescreen. Repeat the message every day, knocking one off the countdown, till she gets in touch. She can't ignore it – not if she's human."

"I can confirm that she is human," Malc replied.

"Thanks. Just send the message."

"Transmitting."

Chapter Fifteen

Luke's plan to prick Sadie's conscience worked. But it took two days before she appeared on Luke's telescreen and asked to meet him face-to-face.

"It's Thursday," Luke replied, talking towards her image in his hotel room. "I've only got nine days. By that, I mean Everton's got nine days. Just tell me what you know right now and I can get on with it."

Sadie shook her head. "I can't be sure you're the only one listening to what I say."

"How do you mean?"

"This signal could be intercepted by... anyone."

Luke sighed. "All right. I'll set out now. Where do you want to meet?"

"Well, I'm not at work today. I really like the Design Gallery in Chesterfield. I'll see you outside it, if that's okay with you."

"I'll find it."

"You can't miss it. Just look for the spire."

Luke understood Sadie's remark when he stood on the green outside the gallery. Straining his neck, he gazed at the enormous tapered tower that pointed towards the heavy sky. The spire did not merely narrow to a high pinnacle. The structure spiralled spectacularly as well, like a helter-skelter at a fairground. The rest of the building was just as chaotic. The stained glass windows were irregular shapes dotted haphazardly on the dark stone walls that bulged outwards imposingly. The whole place seemed to capture the spirit of an architect's outrageous dream. It was impressive, bizarre and disturbing at the same time.

Luke almost jumped when Sadie walked up behind him. "The famous twisted spire," she murmured, as if in awe of the design.

"The whole thing's pretty warped."

"Mmm. Nice."

"Do you want to go in?" asked Luke.

Sadie pointed to a bench, positioned on the lawn for the gallery's admirers.

With his gloved hand, Luke wiped away most of the cold water collected on the wooden slats of the bench. Then he turned to Malc. "Use your laser to evaporate the rest, please."

Malc did not grumble about the misuse of his functions. Instead he swept an intense laser beam over the bench until it was dry and warm.

Once Luke and Sadie had both sat down and cast their eyes again over the misshapen building, Luke turned towards her. He was eager to hear whatever she had to say. "Well? No one's eavesdropping here. And Malc's still not sending details to The Authorities."

Sadie frowned. "How did you manage that?"

"Never mind. There's something more important. You want to tell me about Camilla Bunker."

Sadie shook her head. "Not really. I want to tell you about someone else. A man I knew a few years back. Another computer high-flier. We could have been paired but... it didn't work out like that. Anyway, we... er... shared a dislike for a few things, like the way identity cards rule so much of our lives."

Anxious to get to the point, Luke interrupted. "So you decided to buck the system."

"We worked out what to do together. You know. We agreed what we'd do and what we wouldn't. It was a matter of deciding what's a good reason to help someone in a crisis and what isn't."

"Like a wife wanting to get away from a no-good partner?"

Sadie nodded. "I only help people with a good cause. They promise *never* to mention me and I promise never to say who they are. More than that, I'll do my best to forget all about them after I've changed their identity cards, especially if I've given someone a new name. And, of course, I never keep a record. That's the deal. It's the only way it can work. Mutual trust."

"Mollie Gazzo broke that trust. She told me about you."

"Yes, but she's the only one and The Authorities probably forced her into it somehow."

"Camilla Bunker broke another sort of trust," Luke said to her. "You're trying to help women beat stupid rules and turn a negative into a positive. That's one thing. Helping Camilla get away with murder is something else. The law against killing isn't a stupid rule, is it? She took advantage of you."

"No, she didn't."

"Oh?"

"I've been racking my brains since you told me about that boy in prison. I don't know anyone called Camilla Bunker. Never did. That's why I decided to contact Lee McArthur. He went to Glasgow..."

Interrupting, Luke queried, "Lee McArthur?"

"My old friend. He designed computer systems for transport. We kept in touch for a while after he moved."

"Designed? Past tense?"

Sadie nodded gloomily. "I wouldn't have let on about him but it doesn't matter any more, I guess. His partner — Farrah — told me he died two years ago. She sounded heartbroken — even after all this time."

"What's he got to do with it?"

"I told you how I operate because Lee was doing exactly the same in Glasgow."

"Ah. You're wondering if he gave Camilla a new life."

"I asked Farrah if she knew anything, but she didn't. That was part of our code as well. We told no one what we were up to."

"How did Lee die?" Luke said. "Did you ask?"

"It was a terrible accident. He was electrocuted in the bathroom at home."

At once, Luke's spine tingled and he sat on the edge of the bench. "Electrocuted?"

"Yes. Why?"

"Because Camilla Bunker was an electrician," Luke replied. Suddenly eager to get a fast cab to Glasgow, he stood up. "If she got a new identity from Lee McArthur, she might've made sure he'd never be able to tell anyone her new name."

Thanking Sadie hurriedly, Luke headed for the nearest freeway reader with his identity card ready in his hand.

While the electric cab swerved through the rugged Lake District, Luke said, "Flight GGW17. The plane that crashed. Was it on its way to Glasgow?"

"Correct," Malc answered. "London-to-Glasgow is not a regular service because London is not a popular point of departure. That is why the plane was not full. The airport is in west London, part of The Authorities' regeneration scheme for Hounslow."

"That's where they're building a new sports stadium, accommodation and that sort of thing, to host the International Youth Games, isn't it?"

"Yes. Hounslow Airport was constructed as a convenient destination for overseas athletes and their supporters. It is still open, but its aircraft maintenance centre was closed shortly after the accident."

"So, Camilla had a Glasgow connection. Interesting." Luke was beginning to see several strands coming together like spokes meeting at the hub of a wheel. "She worked in the transport industry, like Lee McArthur. She was an electrician and he designed computer systems, so she might well have come across him through her work. And if she found out what he did on the side… She would've told him she was on the run from a dreadful partner. She wouldn't have said anything about hurting him."

"Speculation," Malc said.

"You're getting seriously predictable, you know," Luke replied.

"All computer-based systems react in a logical and hence predictable way in a given situation. That is a strength, in contrast with the erratic behaviour of humans."

Luke laughed. "Now you're getting competitive!" He was on a high because he thought that he was closing in on the real killer. He had no idea what more he could learn in Glasgow, but there was always a chance that Lee McArthur had left a crumb of evidence. Luke needed every morsel to clinch the case and free an innocent boy before he was put down like a dangerous animal. "I'm sure it should be Camilla Bunker — or whatever she's called now — facing execution, not Everton."

If Malc could have sighed with frustration, he would have done so. But a machine never felt frustrated. "Your theory remains illogical and unlikely. If the prime suspect is innocent, you must explain why he was present at the crime scene and why he contaminated it so extensively."

Brought back down to earth, Luke nodded. "I know. I'm still trying to figure that out." For a while, he watched a yacht slicing through Ullswater. It was chilly outside but not quite cold enough to freeze the whole lake. Along its edge, ice lay like broken panes of glass. The surrounding hillside was patchily white, but it was no longer snowing. "There's one thing that occurs to me. Just maybe... Malc, see if you can get me a speech-only link to the prison doctor, if Cambridge has got one. I suppose they must have."

The cab zoomed past Carlisle and brushed the end of Solway Firth before Malc made a successful connection to Dr Lackie. His voice was beamed into the cab through Malc.

"FI Harding. What can I do for you?"

"I'm interested in Everton Kohter..."

The prison doctor cut him short. "I know. I've got one of the warders with me here – Greg Roper – and he's told me about your visit last week. By coincidence, you've caught us double-checking the doses of the drugs that'll be used to pass sentence. I'm approving the volumes that are appropriate for Kohter's weight and age. Being a

119

doctor, I can't cause a death, but it'll be my duty to pronounce life extinct."

Luke shuddered. Doctors were supposed to save lives, not assist in the taking of life. Dr Lackie did not seem to have any emotional involvement. He talked like a mobile aid to law and crime or a clinical murderer. In a way, he was a clinical murderer, along with Greg Roper. He also seemed to think that an investigator would be equally unaffected emotionally, yet fascinated by the technical detail of the execution.

"Just one question," Luke said, keeping it brief. "Does Everton suffer from epilepsy, by any chance? Does he have fits?"

Dr Lackie's response was immediate. "No. Definitely not. I assess the health of all our prisoners very thoroughly prior to execution. I've had him under observation for the standard two years now and fits are one thing I check very carefully. We don't want a commotion in the Death Cell."

The whole business was far too serious to be funny but Luke saw a grim humour in the doctor's answer. He made it sound as if the prison would execute only people who were well. Luke got the impression that, if Everton had been ill, the death sentence would have been delayed so that he could be cured before he was killed. "Does he have any health problems?"

"Absolutely not. He's in good physical shape. As for his

mental state, depression's normal for someone in his situation. There's little I can do about that."

"Thanks," Luke replied. "That's all." As soon as Malc broke the link, Luke muttered, "An epileptic fit was a good idea. If he'd thrashed around, it would have explained why Everton was covered in blood and bruises and left so much evidence. He might even have made that bite mark and dribbled over Rowan without knowing a thing about it."

"Irrelevant. The prisoner does not have epilepsy and it would not explain why he was present at the murder scene."

It was clear that Everton had played a part in the killing of Rowan Pearce. While Luke did not understand that role, he was still not satisfied that Everton had actually committed the crime. Yet, if Everton had simply been a witness or if he'd intervened in a failed attempt to stop the murder, why had he never said so? Luke sighed and shook his head. Changing his line of inquiry, he asked, "What's on file about Lee McArthur's death?"

Malc had already accessed the database remotely. "No suspicious circumstances were noted in the coroner's report. The mains wiring of the automatic sampler in the smart toilet had become dangerously worn with the result that its metal parts became electrically live. When the subject flushed the toilet, he received a fatal shock through the hand. In the damp conditions of a bathroom, the current was sufficient for the muscles to go into spasm, preventing voluntary release of the metal fitting. The right hand showed typical spark burns, a scorched palm and collapsed blisters. Death resulted from ventricular fibrillation caused by the action of the electrical current on the heart muscle and conducting system."

"Was there any evidence that someone had tampered with the mains supply?"

"No."

"Was there a proper investigation or did they just assume it was bad luck?"

"There is no record of a forensic examination."

"Mmm. Makes me wonder," said Luke as he turned to watch more of the north slip past the window.

Chapter Sixteen

"When I shut my eyes," Farrah said with a pained expression on her face, "I can still see his hand. It was burnt black and purple, and the skin gaped open on his forefinger and thumb. It was hideous. I don't want to..." Her whole body shook and she muttered, "I wish I could forget."

Luke had to admit that pairing worked well for most couples. It was clear that, even after two years, Farrah Bruce was still devastated by the loss of her partner. Sometimes, he wondered if he and Jade were alone in despising the system. But the stormy relationship between Rowan Pearce and Camilla Bunker told him that they weren't the only ones. "I'm sorry," Luke said quietly and inadequately to Farrah. "Did a forensic investigator turn up?"

"It's all a bit of a blur but... no. I came home from work and found him in the bathroom. Awful. Absolutely awful. You can't imagine..." She sniffed and composed herself. "A man came and said it was wear and tear in the insulation and the live wire got exposed. Something like that." Then, struck by a thought, she paused and stared at Luke. Her anguish turned rapidly to horror. "What are you saying? It *was* an accident, wasn't it? Or do you think someone... Is that why everyone's interested again?"

Puzzled by her choice of words, Luke asked, "Everyone? How do you mean?"

"An old colleague called about him as well."

"Who would that be?"

"Erm... a woman in Derby. Sadie something."

Luke nodded. "Kershaw."

"Yes. She didn't know... what had happened to him. I think she was upset. But you're different. You're an FI."

"Yes, but I'm here to get up to running speed, not because I'm ahead of everyone else," he replied. "I wanted to ask, did you know about his... um... unofficial business?"

"Do *you*?"

"He altered identity cards, and made new ones."

"He was a clever man," Farrah stated. "A good man."

"I know. He did people favours. I'm sorry to say this but, if the stakes were high enough, there's a chance someone he helped might've wanted to make sure he kept quiet."

Farrah's mouth fell open for a second before she could reply. "That can't be right! He always swore he'd never say a word. Not under any circumstances. He didn't even tell me who came."

"Was he expecting anyone on the day he died?"

She shrugged. "I wouldn't know for sure. It wasn't something we talked about. But, yes, I believe so. He was... a bit on edge. He always was when... you know."

"Where did he do this work?"

Farrah nodded in the direction of a door. "He had a tiny study in there. Nothing special. Just a computer, card-maker and other bits and pieces. I haven't had the heart to clear it out. I've still got all his clothes as well. If I got rid of his things, it'd feel like he'd never been here. That's wrong. I still want a bit of him around."

Luke's heart rate took a leap. "So the study's just as it was?"

"More or less."

Luke rose to his feet eagerly. "Can I take a look?"

Farrah got up and slowly led the way. At the closed door, she hesitated. "Will this get him – his reputation, I suppose – into trouble? It won't damage his memory, will it?"

"No," Luke answered. "The worst that'll happen is The Authorities confiscate his equipment. But it'll help me figure out if there's more to his accident."

Her fingers were clamped around the handle but still she didn't open the door. "And what if there is? Will you tell me? I need to know."

Luke nodded. "I won't hide anything from you. I can promise that."

Farrah gazed into his face for a moment and then nodded. "All right." She drew back the door to her partner's study and turned on the lamp.

It was an unremarkable and narrow room. On the

right, there was a work surface containing a printer and a computer that had been state-of-the-art three years ago. Luke had never seen the third device before but he realized that it was a forger's way of duplicating the physical appearance of identity cards. The wall opposite the door had a small window of frosted glass so that no one could look in on Lee's privacy. On the left, there was a radiator and a shelf with instruction manuals, a camera and a few trinkets scattered along it.

"Malc," Luke said in a respectful whisper, "do a very fine scan of everything. I'm looking for any traces at all, especially fingerprints with a scar." Then he turned to Farrah who remained in the doorway. "I want to turn his computer and camera on and get my mobile to copy their contents. All right?"

She nodded.

He pushed the button on the processor and said to Malc, "Full download, please." He switched on the camera and put it next to the computer. "That too."

"Tasks logged."

Farrah said, "I'll tell you now, though, he never made a record of names or kept photos, if that's what you're after. He used to jot a few things down here." She tapped a small pad at the end of the work surface. "But he always shredded what he'd written afterwards."

Luke donned latex gloves and made for the jotter. The top page was blank but, if Lee had written on the sheet above, he might have left an impression on it. Luke was not sure if any indentations would last for two years. He picked up the pad and examined it closely, tilting it so that he could look at it from an oblique angle. He was trying to position the page so that the light would cast a shadow into any scoring, making it visible. Seeing indistinct marks was like hearing the murmur of a distant conversation without being able to distinguish the incriminating words. After a minute, Luke shrugged in frustration and put the pad of paper back down on the table. "There's something here, I think, Malc. It's very faint, but I want to know what he wrote. Use your best electrostatic enhancement and document analysis."

"My systems are fully occupied with scanning and downloading. I will process the additional task when I have spare resource."

"Fair enough."

"My scan for fingerprints would be improved by laser enhancement."

"All right." Luke added, "Spray fluorescent dye around as well if it helps, but analyse the pad first. If solvent from the spray gets onto the paper, it'll ruin the electrostatic detection of any impressions."

Malc replied coolly, "I am equipped with programs for deducing the optimum order of given tests."

"Yeah. Sorry. I'll leave you to get on with your job." Luke switched off the lamp, left the study, and pulled the door shut to protect Farrah's eyes and his own from the intense laser beam.

"How long's this going to take?" asked Farrah.

"A few minutes," Luke replied. "Not long. He's an advanced model."

"Do you want a drink while you wait? I make a hot punch with fruit and herbs. Perfect for this weather."

"Mmm. Sounds good. Thanks."

She smiled weakly. "Lee's version was always better than mine, but…" She shrugged and disappeared into the kitchen.

Outside, a monstrous square crane on the other side of the Clyde was lifting goods from an auto-barge onto Stobcross Quay. Seagulls were screaming and diving over scraps in the water. Luke strolled around the living room and realized how much his job of forensic investigator had taken over his life. Most visitors would perhaps admire the view over the river and the city, the quality of the furnishings or the strange collection of coloured-glass bottles. Luke was a scientific observer. He always looked for dust and stray hairs and surfaces that would hold fingerprints. Out of habit, no matter where he was, he wondered what he would sample if he had to uncover what had happened in the room. His forensic brain hardly ever turned off.

He opened the door to the bathroom and looked inside. It was ordinary, clean and reeked of bleach.

Nothing like a crime scene. Closing the door again, Luke reminded himself that Lee had died two years ago. It was highly unlikely that the bathroom or living room retained traces of his death. The study was different because it had remained untouched.

When Farrah returned, she was carrying a tray with two tumblers of a steaming drink, the colour of red wine. It filled the room with the fragrance of spices. Holding the tray towards him, she said, "Watch out. The glass will be hot. But it's best to drink it as warm as you can stand."

"Thanks." Gingerly, he took the drink and sat down. He held the fruit punch under his nose and breathed in the fumes. "Mmm. Nice." Then he glanced at the study door, eager to hear Malc's findings. Looking back to Farrah, he asked, "The first time you went in the study after Lee died, did you notice anything odd?"

"Like what?"

Luke shrugged. "An unusual smell, something out of place, maybe two glasses in the study rather than one, anything."

Farrah sipped her drink. "Not that I recall," she answered.

Following her lead, he tried the drink. Its flavour struck his mouth and shocked him with its intensity. When the liquid trickled down his throat, he let out a little gasp of pleasure. It was like a very hot version of pomegranate juice with added herbs.

"Good?" Farrah said.

"More than that. I ought to get you to download the recipe into my mobile."

From the study, Malc's neutral voice called, "Tasks completed."

Luke jumped up and opened the door, allowing Malc to float out. "What have you got?"

"Very little relevant information," he replied. "The camera's memory has been deleted. The computer does not contain significant data. There are no fingerprints or other biological traces of a third person."

"So, the last one to go in with him was very careful. Hat and gloves at the minimum. What about fibres?"

"There are several. I cannot identify those that originate from visitors without a comparison with all clothing possessed two years ago by Lee McArthur and Farrah Bruce."

Farrah put down her tumbler. "I've still got Lee's, but I've changed a lot of mine."

"Pity." Thinking for a moment, Luke took another drink of the fruit punch. Then he said to Malc, "Before we go, you can sample Farrah and Lee's clothes. Any fibres from the study that don't match must have come from clothes Farrah's thrown out or from someone else. Could still be useful."

"Task logged."

Impatient to hear about the most promising lead, Luke

asked, "What did you make of the pad?"

"The indentions are unclear. I cannot read out the result because there are several possible interpretations of the letters."

Disappointed, Luke sighed. "Can you put an image of them on the telescreen right now?"

"Confirmed."

"Go on, then." Talking to Farrah, he said, "You're familiar with Lee's writing so you might be able to help me work it out."

Farrah nodded. "Okay."

Malc projected a grossly magnified result of his document analysis on the large screen. The result was a grey rectangle with vague and scratchy black lines representing the impressions left on the pad.

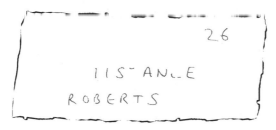

In the top right corner, Luke could make out two digits. The number – 26 – grabbed his attention because it was the clearest impression amid the indistinct scribbles and because it was Camilla's age at the time of Rowan's murder and the plane crash.

Underneath, there were two lines of capital letters.

The first row was very patchy. Making out what had been jotted was like trying to recognize a tune playing against white noise. There was certainly an *S* and then a gap followed by *AN*. After another unidentifiable letter, an *E* appeared.

The second line was clearer. Luke felt a tingle as he picked out the surname of *ROBERTS*. He turned to Farrah and asked, "First, is it Lee's writing?"

She swallowed and nodded. "It's hard to see, isn't it? But, yes, that's Lee all right."

The squiggles were the ghostly echo of Lee McArthur's last written words.

"What do you make of it? Apart from the twenty-six, what does it say?"

Farrah got up and walked up to the telescreen. "Not sure." She peered at the muddled scrawl and said, "It's an *N* or *M* before the *S*." She traced the hazy lines with her forefinger. "If it's an *M*, you've got *MS*. As in Ms Farrah Bruce."

Suddenly, Luke became tense. "Yeah. It's someone Roberts, isn't it?"

She nodded in agreement. "The first name's *A*, *N*, something, *E*."

"It's got to be Anne, hasn't it?" Luke said.

"I can't make out another *N* but, yes, I don't know what else it could be."

Luke was up on his feet, gazing intently at the faint

black marks blending into the dark background. "I suppose it could be Angie — there's a sort-of curve that could be a *G* — but I don't think there's enough room for two letters in there. No. It's more likely to be Anne. Ms Anne Roberts." He turned towards his mobile and issued an urgent command. "Search all available databases, Malc. Highest priority. I want a list of everyone called Anne Roberts."

"Processing."

Turning back to Farrah, Luke said, "Does the name of Anne Roberts mean anything to you?"

She shook her head. "No."

"It could be the name Lee gave to his last client before... you found him. So she might be able to throw some light on what happened to him."

Sadly, Farrah mumbled, "I just wish I knew where all this was heading."

Sympathetically, Luke replied, "I'll tell you when I've got something to report. Right now, I want to let Malc loose in your wardrobes. All right? After that, I can leave you alone."

"Fine." She led the way to the bedroom.

Chapter Seventeen

"There are two hundred and thirteen people called Anne Roberts, according to The Authorities' files," Malc reported.

Trying not to be put off by the large number, Luke said, "And how many are twenty-seven to twenty-nine years old now?"

"Eleven."

"That's better. If Camilla Bunker survived the crash and killed her husband, she did it to escape her life in the south. How many of those Anne Roberts live north of Coventry?"

"Six."

"Camilla – or Anne – would've settled somewhere in the last two years. Take away all those known to have been in their current homes or jobs for 3 years or more."

"One remaining."

Luke smiled at last. "Bob's your uncle! Plot a route to wherever she is, Malc. Where are we going?"

"Newcastle."

"Mmm. Very nice. On the way, you'd better tell me what you know about Anne Roberts of Newcastle. Is she an electrician?"

"She is listed as a lighting engineer."

"And what do we use to power our lights?"

"Electricity."

"Can this cab go any faster?"

Luke gathered his fleecy coat around him and then pushed his hands deep into his pockets as he sat on the bench outside the riverside apartment block. On the other side of the Tyne, the Concert Hall was the shape of a giant woodlouse. The bridge that carried cabs across the river was a mass of impressive ironwork. Behind and above him was Newcastle's spectacularly jagged skyline. The nearest clock tower belonged to Newcastle School, famed for gun sport.

"You know," Luke said to Malc, narrowing the gap between his forefinger and thumb, "I'm this close to saving Everton Kohter. I've come all this way to interview Anne Roberts and she's not at home." He sighed. "Are you sure I can't go into her flat and look around?"

"You can enter almost any property if you have significant evidence that the owner is involved in a crime. You have no such evidence against Anne Roberts."

"I might if I get into her apartment."

"It would be an illegal entry," Malc insisted.

Luke nodded. "I know. It's a matter of civil liberty. It'd be a way of getting warm, though." He glanced at Malc and added, "You don't feel the cold, do you? You don't know what it's like."

"I can tolerate a wide range of operating temperatures. My systems will work down to fifty degrees below zero."

"And you wouldn't even shiver."

"Shivering brings warmth to a human's outer surface. It would serve no purpose for me."

A jogger left the Tyne Walkway and made for the entrance of the apartment block. At once, Luke got to his feet and called, "Excuse me."

The man came to a halt in a little cloud created by his own panting. "Yes?" he said, clearly out of breath after his run and startled that an FI should stop him.

"I'm looking for Anne Roberts. Do you know her?"

He nodded. "My place is a couple of doors along from hers."

"Would you call her a friend?"

He shrugged. "I suppose so. She's all right."

"How long's she been living here?"

"A year? No. More like two."

"She's not at home right now. Any idea where she might be?"

The runner glanced at his watch. "Maybe she's still at work."

Luke shook his head. Malc had already contacted her employer and discovered that she was not on duty.

"She's into fitness. Try the Waterside Skills and Fitness Club. Just down there." The man pointed along the walkway that ran parallel to the river. "Two or three minutes on foot."

"Thanks." Luke took off with Malc in his wake.

Newcastle had been built on two different levels. Along the grand waterfront, there was a series of restaurants, hotels, clubs and small apartment blocks overlooking the Tyne. On the higher ground behind, the main part of the fabulous city towered over everything.

Luke soon found the club and showed his identity card at the reception. "Is Anne Roberts in at the moment?" he enquired.

The receptionist studied a monitor for a few moments and then replied, "Yes. Room 14, it says here. Next floor up. You can't miss it. Look for the long see-through wall." He hesitated before adding mysteriously, "Be very careful if you go in."

Luke walked down a corridor, squash courts on one side, indoor tennis on the other. By the general gymnasium, there was an elevator. He went up one storey and came out in another warm and wide passageway. On his left, some members were playing a darts tournament. The glass window of Room 14 was on his right. Inside, there were two long alleys. A middle-aged man occupied one and a stern-looking woman in her twenties stood in the other. Both were throwing knives at separate targets. There was a red warning light on the door and a sign that read *Danger: No entry*.

Luke watched the concentration on the woman's face as a vicious blade flew from her hand. Spinning rapidly, it sliced through the air and, a moment later, pierced the centre of a wooden target. It was all over in a flash. Luke could not hear the thud of the knife hitting its target but he watched the steel shaft quiver with the energy that she'd put into the throw. A second or two later, its vibrations damped down and the woman looked towards the uninvited spectator.

Luke beckoned to her.

She turned and said something to the other member of the club and then made for the corridor. As soon as she swiped her identity card and opened the door, the red light and the warning notice disappeared. Staring at Luke, she said, "Yes?"

"Anne Roberts?" he asked.

"That's me," she replied tersely, as if annoyed that he'd interrupted her practice.

She had thin lips, a severe nose, tied-back bundles of hair, and a lean neck. Her wiry features gave her a harsh appearance. And she still had a knife in her hand.

"Put the weapon away, please," Luke said. "My mobile might get nervous and zap you."

She glared at him for a second and then reluctantly slipped it into a leather carrier around her waist.

"Right." He showed her his identity card and then said, "Can I see yours, please?" He put out his hand. Once Anne had placed her card in his palm, he examined it briefly and then held it out so Malc could scan it.

"What is this?" she demanded to know.

Ignoring her question, Luke returned her identity card. "Now your hands, please. Hold them up."

She did not follow his instruction. Instead, she glanced at Malc before remarking, "You're young to be an FI."

"Yes, but you still have to do what I say. Palms outwards

so I can see your fingers and my mobile can record your prints."

She raised her eyebrows and sighed but held up her hands in a gesture of surrender.

As soon as Malc had completed his scan, Luke looked at her fingers closely. He could not see a scar. Not even a tiny one. And there was no sign of cosmetic surgery.

"You're good with knives," he observed.

She put her hands down, placing them at the ready on her sports belt. "It requires discipline – it sharpens the mind – but it's a form of relaxation at the same time."

"Where did you live before you came to Newcastle?"

"Why are you asking? What's going on?"

"It's nothing," Luke replied. "Just a possible technical issue with your identity card. So, where did you live?"

"London, but I'm not proud of it."

"Whereabouts in London?"

"Hounslow."

It was the location of the airport and an up-and-coming sports venue, kilometres away from where Camilla Bunker and Rowan Pearce used to live, but not far enough to provide a firm alibi.

Heart thumping, Luke turned to Malc and asked the most important question. "Do the prints you've just recorded match any others in this case?"

"No."

Luke was taken aback by Malc's abrupt answer.

"No?" Luke checked.

"Correct. They are grossly different from any in the crime scene file."

Luke's idea had collapsed even before he'd begun to put pressure on Anne Roberts. Her fingerprints proved that she could not be Camilla Bunker. More importantly, Luke's idea for saving Everton Kohter had collapsed as well. He tried not to give the impression of being disappointed, but inwardly he groaned.

Spitefully, Anne said, "Looks like you've finished with me. Looks like you never had a technical issue to resolve. And I've got training to do."

Luke nodded. "Yes. Thanks. That's all."

Back in Sheffield, gazing at his own personal planetarium projected by Malc, Luke shook his head. "This theory about Camilla Bunker is the only thing coming between Everton and the sword that's hanging over him."

"Incorrect," Malc said. "Everton Kohter will be executed by lethal injection."

"Yes. All right. But that's not my point. I thought I was on the right track with Anne Roberts but she hasn't got any skeletons in her cupboard."

Malc replied, "You did not have legal access to her living quarters so I was unable to scan inside her furniture."

Luke sighed and said, "I think you're programmed to do this to me on purpose. Open dictionary. Skeleton in the cupboard means hiding a guilty secret."

"Entered."

"I just don't know where the logic went wrong."

"The interpretation of the impressions on the pad of paper was far from certain."

Luke nodded. "I'll show it to my assistant investigator tomorrow. See what she makes of it."

"You do not have an…"

"My *unofficial* assistant. Jade."

"She is not trained in forensic techniques. There is no reason to believe that she will decipher the impressions differently."

"There's no reason to believe she'll see it like I did either. No harm in giving her a go."

Chapter Eighteen

Luke sat beside Jade in her sound studio on Saturday morning and shivered. This time it was pleasure that made him tingle. Her latest electronic piece — a series of unhurried soundscapes — was the perfect antidote to a murder investigation. Yet, every now and again, there was a disturbing low frequency rumble that seemed to vibrate right through his entire body.

When the music came to an end, Luke looked at her in wonder. "Brilliant! Again."

She laughed. "Not exactly party music. Soothing but a bit unsettling as well, if you know what I mean. Just something I put together in the last few days — while you've been touring around the country, having a holiday."

"A holiday?" he replied, pretending to be annoyed. "If only. The bad guys never take time off so I'm the same. Listening to your stuff now is my biggest holiday. But…"

Jade looked at him with suspicion. "What? Don't tell me you're sitting here with me thinking about a case."

"I wanted you to take a quick look at something and see what you think it says."

"You mean, use my eyes? But I'm a musician. My ears are my strong point."

Luke pointed at the blank wall of the studio. "Beam it up there, Malc." Then he turned back to Jade. "Just have a try. It's a name and I can't quite make it out."

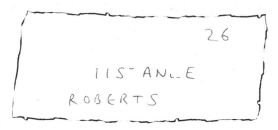

26

I I S¯ A N ∪ E

R O B E R T S

Jade ran her hand through her mostly bronze hair and cocked her head on one side. "Well, there's the number twenty-six at the top. Then it's… someone Roberts."

"Mmm. Have a stab at the first name."

"I don't know. Is it Angie? Or maybe *A*, *N*, *O*, *E*, like the end of canoe, but that doesn't make sense."

Luke nodded. "I thought there was a curly letter after the N as well, but couldn't make anything of it, so I guessed it was Anne."

"Looks more like a *C* to me. As in the end of dance." She shrugged. "There's something before it and then an *S*."

"I thought it might be Ms. Ms Anne Roberts."

Jade stepped back away from the image, shaking her head. "Two things wrong with that. You could write Ms Roberts or Anne Roberts so everyone knows you're dealing with a girl or a woman, but why use both? If you say Anne, you don't say Ms as well. That's overkill."

"Good point," said Luke. "What's the other thing that's wrong?"

"Well, the *S* is as big as all the other letters. That's a bit weird. Most people write the *s* smaller than the *M* in Ms."

"Yeah. Maybe it's not Ms after all. But…" He sighed.

"No, I don't know either," Jade told him.

Luke stood at Jade's side, his arm brushing hers, but concentrated on the image. "You know, there's something strange. The lines are unbalanced."

"What do you mean?" Jade asked.

"If you write a name in capital letters on a small pad like that, you more-or-less centre the words on the page. Don't you? I think so. The *ROBERTS* is shifted over to the left. You'd expect the E to be in the middle of the page because it's the middle of Roberts, but it isn't. Look. It's centred on the *R*. There's four letters to the left of it and only two on its right. Maybe there's a couple of letters after *ROBERTS* to balance everything up, but I'm not seeing them."

"Nor me," Jade added, "but I can guess. If there's a hidden *O* and *N*, you've got Robertson."

Luke glanced at her and nodded. "It's not just good ears you've got. Your other bits aren't bad." He turned back to the white wall serving as a screen for the impression analysis. "The first line's off-centre as well. You've got the four letters of Anne – or five of Angie or whatever it is – on the right, and just MS or something on the left. Maybe it's part of a longer name. If that's right, I reckon there's a couple of letters missing on the left. You'd need them to balance the line. What are the possibilities, Malc?"

The mobile searched a database of names and said, "There is no known female name with *MS* in that position."

"Perhaps it's not an *M*," Luke replied. "Farrah thought it might be an *N*, so let's try it. We'd have: blank, blank, possible *N*, *S*, blank, *A*, *N*, a curly letter maybe, then *E*."

"I'll stick to music," Jade muttered, tired of peering at the faint doodles.

"Malc, try to fill in the gaps. What fits?"

It took Malc only sixteen seconds. "There is only one viable solution," he said. "The female name of Constance would fit the impressions."

Luke beamed. "Now I'm getting somewhere. Check surnames as well, Malc. Are there any options other than Robertson?"

"Robertson is the only surname of that length. You may wish to consider the possibility of Robertshaw."

"All right. Do a complete search for anyone called Constance Robertson or Constance Robertshaw, twenty-seven to twenty-nine years old, living north of Coventry since the plane crash." While Malc consulted The Authorities' files, Luke faced Jade and said, "Thanks. I reckon this forger in Glasgow gave Camilla Bunker a new identity. He jotted down what she wanted to be called – and her age – while he faked her card. This," he said, waving at the scored image of the pad, "is what's left of his writing."

Jade smiled. "Great idea to call yourself Constance when it means something that doesn't change."

"Search completed," Malc announced. "Within the parameters you set, there is only one person. Constance Robertson is an electrician, twenty-eight years old, living in Ballachulish."

Luke punched the air. "Fantastic. Where's Ballachulish?"

"It is an isolated village in the Highlands. It is on the bank of Lake Leven at the far end of the Pass of Glencoe."

Luke cut short his celebration. "That's what I call north," he said with a groan.

"From here, the journey will take between four hours thirty minutes and seven hours by cab."

Looking puzzled, Luke asked, "Why so uncertain?"

"In winter, the Pass of Glencoe is often blocked by snowfall."

Eagerly, Luke said, "Request a snowplough, then, because Ballachulish is where we're going. I can't wait to interview her."

"You will have to wait a minimum of four and a half hours," Malc replied.

Jade merely giggled.

The cab went slowly past a mountain rescue unit, over a river and entered the Pass of Glencoe. A corridor with pure white walls had been carved out of ice and snow. The roof of the cab completed the feeling of going into a cave.

Only the murky daylight told Luke that he wasn't completely enclosed.

Making Luke jump, Malc started to speak with the voice of The Authorities. "FI Luke Harding. We are positive about your potential as a forensic investigator but we were expecting more progress in the Sheffield corruption case." The voice sounded frustrated and maybe even annoyed. It was also crackly. The interference was probably a result of distance and the weather conditions.

Straightaway, Luke was on his guard. "I'm making a lot of progress..."

The voice interrupted. "There has been very little feedback from your mobile aid to law and crime. There can only be two reasons for this. Either the case is not advancing as well as you say or your mobile is faulty. Its self-diagnostic programs are not reporting faults."

Luke had no option but to lie. He hoped that a logic circuit somewhere in Malc would work out why and not correct him. "I'm getting plenty of evidence but it isn't the sort that can go in case notes. Once I get good physical evidence, I'll wrap it up pretty quickly, I think."

Luke held his breath but, much to his relief, Malc didn't contradict him. His mobile must have figured out that correcting him would have revealed their suspicions that The Authorities were guilty of incitement to commit a crime.

"Very well," the voice said. "Continue. But if the situation does not improve soon, we will recall your mobile aid to law and crime for an extensive service."

Luke knew what that meant. It was a threat. The Authorities would extract all of the data from Malc's memory. They could delete anything that they didn't like. Luke feared that, when Malc was released to continue his duties, any incriminating evidence would have been erased.

The cab slowed to a crawl to take a tight bend. On Luke's left, there was still some flowing water. The stream came over a ridge, rolled over a massive bulge made of merged icicles and fell into a hole in the snow below. Somewhere under the white covering, there must have been a liquid pool. Beyond the frozen ridge, Luke could see the imposing mountains, cloaked in snow. The mountaintops were much whiter and brighter than the grey sky that lumbered above them.

He turned towards Malc and said, "Can you get me a link to Sadie Kershaw? She's got very powerful computers. I want you to download a copy of all your information on the Pairing Committee corruption case into one of her systems. She can keep it just in case you're... serviced."

"Your request is highly unconventional."

"Is it illegal?"

"The law does not cover this eventuality. Attempting to

gain unauthorized access to my data is illegal. Giving it away was not considered a possibility."

"So, it's legal," Luke replied.

"It is certainly against the spirit of the law, but it is not expressly forbidden."

"If it makes you happier, protect the file with high-level security. Then only you and me can get into it. No one can fiddle with it."

"I do not experience…"

"Yes, all right. You're never happy. But contact Sadie and let's get it sorted out. She'll agree because it's to her advantage. Proving The Authorities have acted illegally is the only way she'll get off a charge of forgery. She can claim she was forced to do it by Mollie Gazzo acting on behalf of The Authorities. Clear incitement."

"Attempting to establish a connection."

The cab continued to weave between the snowbound mountains. If it had been moving at full speed, it would have felt like a bobsleigh hurtling through an icy channel. But it was maddeningly slow as it began the long descent towards the village of Ballachulish. At least the extended journey gave Malc enough time to link with Sadie Kershaw and transmit the corruption case notes into a spare processor in Derby.

Half an hour later, the mountains rolled back from the corridor and the view opened up in front of Luke. All of a sudden, the isolated village appeared on his left and the glassy lake on his right. This far north, it was so cold that the stretch of water was partly frozen. The electric cab pulled into the station and ground to a halt. Luke wrapped himself up in a thick coat and said, "Okay, Malc. Take me to Constance Robertson's address."

There was a picturesque triangle of solid stone-built cottages. No high-rise here. The houses seemed to be squatting down to shelter from the worst of the highland weather. Malc glided through the light snowfall and Luke crunched the fallen snow under his boots until they came to a halt by Constance Robertson's door.

Even after the third push of the old-fashioned doorbell, no one answered. Luke shook his head miserably and stamped his feet to keep the chill from his toes. It was turning out just like the visit to Anne Roberts' empty quarters in Newcastle.

Giving up for the moment, Luke trudged to the hamlet's restaurant. Grateful to be indoors again, he ordered a meal and asked the owner, "Do you know Constance Robertson?"

The woman behind the counter chuckled. "You come from a town or city, don't you? In a place like Ballachulish, it goes without saying that everyone knows each other."

"When did she move here?"

"Two years ago. Sticks out like a sore thumb."

"Why's that?"

"She's a newcomer. That's all. She's not one of us."

Luke nodded. "Do you get on with her?"

The woman looked him in the eye. "I just said. She's not one of us."

"Do you know where she is?"

"That's another thing. Everyone knows where everyone else is, particularly in this weather. I have to admit she's making the most of being here. Yachting on the lake, hill walking, working in Fort William, skiing. She'll help anyone with an electrical problem. She's been a boon like that. But…"

"She's an outsider who doesn't belong," Luke suggested.

"Aye. And an awkward customer. She's willing to help out, but folk say they don't like her. She's never said much about her past, either. Only that she didn't like it down south but loves being up here."

"So, where is she right now?" asked Luke.

"She took the ferry to Fort William. She was having a weekend skiing. That's what she said."

Luke sighed. "Skiing. So now I've got to chase her up – or down – a mountain."

"What's she done?"

"Oh, I don't know. Like you," Luke replied, "I just want to talk to her about her past." He shrugged. "It's probably nothing. Just a formality, you know."

For some reason, the restaurant owner smiled and

nodded at him. "Enough said. I'll go and get your dinner."
Plainly, she'd somehow decided that Luke's sly words had
confirmed all her doubts about an outsider.

Luke turned to Malc and said, "You'd better book me
into a hotel."

Chapter Nineteen

Luke woke with a start in Fort William on Sunday morning. He thought that he'd heard something like the chilling whoosh of a gust of wind or the slicing of a sword through air. He jolted, sat up in bed, and shivered. "Brr. It's freezing in here!"

"Technically, you are wrong. It is ten point seven degrees," Malc told him. "That is cold for a human being."

"What's going on?"

"I have been informed that the hotel's heating system has broken down."

"Well, fire your laser – low power – at my clothes for a bit. Can you warm them up a bit without burning them?"

"It is improper use of my sophisticated system, but it is possible."

"Just do it, Malc. I want to get up, not freeze to death."

The date glimmering at the bottom of the telescreen was Sunday 5th February. As soon as Luke saw it, he realized why his imagination had conjured up a swishing blade. It was exactly a week until the execution of Everton Kohter and Luke still had a picture of a sword hanging over the boy's head. The figures underneath the date told him that it was 07.21. Still dark outside. Sunrise was about half-an-hour away. Luke shuddered again. The death penalty would be enacted at dawn next Sunday.

While Luke slipped hurriedly into his newly warmed clothes, he thought about the day ahead. Before the sun went down again, he aimed to prove that Rowan Pearce had been murdered by Camilla Bunker, now posing somewhere in Fort William under a false name. He'd failed to find her yesterday. Today, he'd be the first person to arrive at the chair lift on the edge of the town and he'd stay there until a woman called Constance Robertson swiped her identity card through the reader.

In a way, he was grateful to that uncanny dreamlike noise and the cold for waking him. He didn't even complain about the lack of pomegranates on the breakfast menu at the hotel. As quickly as he could, he made a dash for the control room beside the ski slope's chair lift. And there, he waited for his suspect.

He was still waiting after lunch.

Bored and annoyed, Luke reviewed the details of the case in his mind. When he came to think about the downed flight to Glasgow, he saw a parallel with Fort William Hotel this morning. One had a fatal flaw in its fuel line, the other had a crippled heating system. Camilla Bunker had been onboard the aeroplane to advise on its electrical system. Now, she was somewhere in Fort William when the hotel needed an electrician to fix its heating fault. With a queasy feeling in his stomach, Luke realized that his strategy of waiting at the base of the ski slope could be a waste of time and a mistake.

He said, "Contact the hotel, Malc. Have they had an electrician in yet?"

A minute later, Malc replied, "Yes. The heating system is now being tested."

"Who's doing it?"

After another thirty seconds, he answered, "Constance Robertson. She was on call in the town."

Luke muttered under his breath and grabbed his coat. "Come on. We're going back." Out in the open air, he ran through the snow towards the town.

By the time that he reached the hotel desk, though, the electrician had finished the repair and gone. "Where did she go?" he gasped.

The receptionist shrugged. "She wasn't in a good mood, to say the least. I don't think she liked having her weekend interrupted. She said it wasn't worth going skiing any more. I don't know, but I assumed she was just going home."

"Thanks." With that, Luke raced out of the hotel and made for the ferry terminal.

Leaving a trail of misty breath behind him, he sprinted towards Lake Linnhe. Yet, as soon as he reached the waterfront, he knew that he was too late. Three hundred metres ahead, a ferry was pulling away from the main jetty, churning the calm surface of the water. Luke came to a halt and, hands on hips, let out a weary sigh. "This," he said irritably, "is turning into a farce." Trying not to lose heart, he added, "At least we know where she's going."

"The ferry does not have a human captain," Malc told him. "It is piloted by computer."

"What are you saying? Can you take control remotely and bring it back?"

"In principle, yes. However, you do not have sufficient evidence against Constance Robertson to justify such an intervention."

"All right. Can I get back to Ballachulish quickly? Quicker than the ferry would be good." Luke didn't want to waste more time, waiting hours for the boat to return. "How about a cab?"

"At this time of the year, the Lake Leven bridge is impassable. Cabs must take a long detour around the lake to reach Ballachulish. That is why the ferry is popular."

"The mountain rescue people will have a helicopter or two."

"Do you wish to request…"

"No," Luke replied, cutting Malc short. "I know the answer already. 'You do not have sufficient evidence to justify a helicopter.' No chance."

Luke looked up and down the quayside for an alternative. There were several yachts but, with barely a hint of a breeze, they weren't going anywhere. Luke also spotted an old man preparing to go out fishing. His boat looked as rickety as the man himself.

Even so, it was Luke's best bet. He went along the narrow quay, greeted the fisherman, and then nodded towards his boat. "It's seen better days, hasn't it?"

The man stared at Luke in astonishment. He touched the wooden cabin tenderly, his hand coming to rest on an immaculately polished brass rail. "She's got plenty of life left in her," he replied gruffly, as if defending a loved one from a monstrous insult. "Best vessel in Fort William. Believe me."

Luke smiled. "I bet it couldn't beat the ferry to Ballachulish."

The man had wrinkled leathery skin and the white flakes of snow in his hair made him look even older than he really was. He peered round at the receding ferryboat. Then he laughed. "You're wrong, lad. She can still outrun that thing."

Winding him up a bit more, Luke shook his head. "Not a hope."

"Aye. She goes like a youngster."

Luke walked across the gangplank, followed by his mobile aid to law and crime. "Okay. How about showing me? Prove it!"

The man couldn't backtrack now. Crying off would have insulted his treasured boat further. He checked out the distance to the auto-ferry once more and then said, "You're a forensic investigator. What's your name?"

"Luke."

"Tom," he replied. "And you've got yourself a ride on Highlander. Here. Give me a hand with these ropes and I'll show you what she can do."

Untied, the boat chugged slowly backwards, away from the jetty. Once Tom had spun the wheel and turned the prow to the southwest, he engaged full throttle. Maybe Highlander was more used to sedate crossings and lazy fishing expeditions, but it did lift its bow a little and get up some speed.

Luke leaned against the rail near the front. "Hey. You're right," he shouted above the growl of the motor. "It's faster than it looks."

"She's a beauty."

Luke thought of any boat as *it*. He couldn't sense female character in the wood, plastic or metal. There again, someone like Tom might not see Malc as male. Luke's mobile was just a metal machine after all. But referring to Malc as *it* seemed to Luke to be a slur. Like Highlander, though, Malc could not feel insulted.

Luke joined Tom by the wheel where a cover sheltered them from the worst of the weather.

"I hope I'm chasing an international criminal," Tom said with a hearty laugh. "Something I've always fancied doing."

"You're pretty close," Luke replied.

Grinning, he shook his head. "Excellent! Wait till I tell my wife — if she believes me." He beamed at Luke and then added, "I must say, you don't look old enough to be going round chasing international criminals."

Luke smiled. "Between us, we've got the right average age."

Tom hooted with laughter. "Aye. That we have, lad."

Highlander's bow pushed aside floating chunks of ice as it narrowed the gap slightly on the boat in front.

"The ferry's got fancy radar equipment to avoid the bigger lumps of ice. Huh. I've got my eyes," said Tom, spinning the wheel again.

"Has an iceberg ever sunk a boat here?" With a worried frown, Luke watched a large piece of floating ice bob past.

"Once, I remember. A long time ago. It was just a dinghy, not built like Highlander. Or the ferry."

A sudden flurry of snow wiped out Luke's view of the ferryboat's stern for a few seconds. "Just to make sure, Malc, go and sit on the prow and scan for large lumps of ice, will you?"

"Define what you mean by large."

"Big enough to be dangerous to the boat," Luke replied.

Lake Linnhe was two kilometres wide and absolutely straight for as far as Luke could see. It lay in a steep-sided valley, a narrow carving through the mountain range. On either side, thick ice lined the bank. Beyond, there was a narrow strip of evergreens, silvered by snow, and then a rock face. The mountains peaked somewhere above the heavy cloud. The channel made a dramatic straight for a race. Highlander was catching up the auto-ferry, but only slowly, like a distance runner who didn't have the energy for a sprint.

Luke must have looked concerned because Tom said, "She's on schedule, lad. Twenty-five kilometres to Ballachulish. Plenty of time to overtake."

"I'm sorry I conned you into…"

Once again, Tom roared with laughter. "You didn't fool me. I knew what you were up to and I was happy to play along. Aye. Wouldn't have missed it for the world."

Luke wandered out from under the protection of the hood and stood at the brass rail. A couple of snowflakes lodged on his eyelashes and he wiped them away with his gloved fingers. He'd been in a few races, but never on a track like this.

Eventually, Highlander edged closer until it was only a few metres behind. When the lake tapered to a width of about three hundred metres, Luke could feel the ferry's wake rocking Highlander. Coming out of the bottleneck, the waterway opened up again and Lake Leven appeared on the left. Tom steered into it, taking a shorter course than the auto-ferry. Within minutes, Highlander was alongside and it was Tom's boat that got its nose under the snowbound Ballachulish Bridge first.

Tom steered Highlander expertly round a headland

and a small island, blanketed in white, and then headed directly for Ballachulish pier with clear water between his old cherished boat and the modern ferry. Pulling alongside the wooden structure, Tom jumped out as if he were a young man again. "Throw me the rope, lad. And then tell me I've got the best vessel on Lake Leven."

It was Luke's turn to laugh. He hurled the heavy rope towards Tom and shouted, "Agreed. No contest."

Tom tied up his boat, arched his back and put his fists in the cool air. "Victory!"

Behind them, the computerized ferry manoeuvred itself carefully up to the other side of the jetty.

Luke leapt onto dry land and shook Tom's hand. "Thanks. You've been great. Looks like I've got work to do now."

"You go and catch your international criminal, son. I'm going fishing. Then I've got a tale to tell my wife."

As Luke dashed towards the terminal building, he heard Tom's loud cackle behind him.

One by one, passengers from the ferry disembarked and pushed their identity cards against the security panel. In the controller's office, a succession of names appeared on the monitor. With a pounding heart, Luke was looking alternately at the list and the line of travellers.

Eventually, the name of Constance Robertson appeared on the screen and Luke muttered, "That's her!" Looking up, he saw a small severe woman with only the bony features of her face showing out of masses of clothing. She was carrying her skiing gear over her shoulder. Even though she was dressed in many layers, Luke could tell that she was slender. He dashed down the steps from the control room and into the entrance hall.

Constance gasped in surprise as Luke appeared suddenly in front of her.

He held up his identity card and said, "Constance Robertson. I've got a few questions for you."

Chapter Twenty

After unwinding her scarf and peeling off her coat and thick jumper, a slight woman in her late twenties emerged. A sapphire brooch in the shape of a butterfly decorated the coat that she draped over the back of a seat. Her face was not riddled with guilt, Luke noted, but she didn't seem to be puzzled either. If she were innocent, she would have been very curious about an FI who'd travelled such a long way to ask her a few questions. Her manner smacked of confrontation more than curiosity.

Luke took her identity card and let Malc scan it for any imperfections.

Constance adjusted the thermostat setting in her living room and then sat down. "I don't know what this is all about," she said tersely.

"I want you to hold up your hands so my mobile can record your fingerprints," said Luke.

Constance let out a groan. Grudgingly, she did as she was told.

Luke took a good look as well. He could hardly contain himself when he saw her right forefinger. "Can you tell me how you got that scar?" he said, pointing at it.

She examined her fingertip as if she were unaware of any injury. "Oh, that. Just a slip with wire strippers."

"When did it happen?"

163

"No idea. It's not like it's a big thing. Not very memorable."

Malc interrupted. "I have a significant result from fingerprint analysis."

Luke smiled. "Yes?"

"The fingerprints that I have just recorded match precisely those of Camilla Bunker."

"Including the scar?"

"Confirmed."

"What have you entered into case notes?" Luke wanted Constance to hear the conclusion from Malc because she would know that mobiles always told the truth. She would also know that he'd pass the information to The Authorities. Luke hoped to have most impact on her that way.

Malc answered, "There is sure proof that Constance Robertson is Camilla Bunker. Therefore, she survived the air traffic accident. Her identity card is perfect, but it must be forged. The forger was Lee McArthur. Camilla Bunker returned to her house in London after the damage to her finger because a scarred print was found on the work surface of the kitchen."

Luke looked down on Constance Robertson and raised his eyebrows.

She stared back at him without a word. She interlocked her fingers and held them so tightly that the brown skin over her knuckles almost turned white.

Trying to catch her out, Luke said, "On top of that, I

can get Lee McArthur to identify you."

Her expression of disbelief gave her away. "But he's…" She ground to a halt.

"What?"

"Nothing."

Luke smiled again. "You were going to say he's dead, but how would you know that? You had no contact with him after he made your fake card. That was the deal."

After a few more seconds of silence, her resolve cracked. "All right. You've discovered who I am. So what?"

"I'm trying to work out how many offences you've committed."

"Look," she said angrily, "You don't know what it was like with Rowan. He was a slob. I volunteered to go on that plane as part of my work. Anything to take a break from him. And I was coming up here to take a peek at how the other half lives. I didn't get past Coventry as it turned out. But I'd already heard enough. It'd be a leap in my lifestyle. I was hungry for it, wanting to settle in the north but, with Rowan and my old identity card weighing me down, there was no chance. When the plane crashed and I walked away with cuts and bruises, I realized I'd stumbled across a way of disappearing."

"Yes. You wandered off, then went back to leave some clues at the crash site, didn't you? Your pairing ring and identity card."

"Yes," she admitted. "To make sure Rowan and everyone

else thought I was dead."

Luke was on the verge of nailing her for murder but he also sensed that she was clever and slippery. "Why did you go home afterwards?"

"Did I?" she replied with an innocent expression.

"Yes. We've got a print with a scar across it."

"I didn't say when I nicked my finger. It could've been before the plane came down."

"Come on! You walked away with cuts and bruises," Luke said, the disbelief clear in his voice. "I think we know what cut your finger. And it wasn't wire strippers."

"All right. I went back to London to collect a few items." She shrugged, implying that she'd done nothing wrong.

"How did you get there? And how did you go to Glasgow afterwards?"

"I befriended a couple of people who used their cards to call me cabs."

"Was Rowan at home when you got there?"

Camilla hesitated. "No. I went when I knew he'd be out."

Luke understood her strategy. If she admitted that she'd seen him, she'd have a motive for killing him because she couldn't allow anyone to know she was alive. "That's not true, is it? He was there and you murdered him."

She shook her head. "You arrested a boy. I heard the news."

"Yes. You must've been relieved. We're executing him in a week. That doesn't bother you, does it?"

"Why should it? He's a murderer. He deserves what he

gets. Rowan was… a pain, but he didn't deserve that."

Luke shook his head with an ironic smile. "I'll tell you what happened. You went back to make sure Rowan wouldn't come looking for you."

She laughed. "What an imagination! He wouldn't have done that. Not him. And he'd think I was dead. There was no reason for me to kill him."

"There *was* a reason," Luke insisted. "Just disappearing wasn't enough for you. You couldn't resist going back with the ultimate alibi and getting revenge. You hated him so much, you wanted to be rid of him altogether."

She threw up her hands in a gesture of frustration, like an instructor who couldn't get a student to understand a simple idea. "That's stupid!"

"Maybe I'm wrong, then. Maybe you *did* go home to pick up some things. You went when you thought he wouldn't be there, but he was. As soon as he saw you, you knew you had to finish him off to make your scheme work."

"Why don't you ask your mobile if there's proof I killed anyone? Why don't you ask it how many crimes I've committed? One. A forged identity card. And there's extenuating circumstances for that. I had to get away from a useless partner."

Luke didn't have to ask Malc because he already knew the answer. Constance – or Camilla – had admitted that she'd run away from the crash site and got herself a new identity, but he couldn't pin any other offence on her yet.

He could prove only that she'd been at the murder scene, not that she was the one who had stabbed Rowan Pearce. The impressions on the pad were evidence that she'd also been to Lee McArthur's apartment. She wasn't denying it, so he didn't need to match the fibres from Lee's study with her clothing. But knowing that she'd been there wasn't proof that she'd sabotaged his electrical supply. After all this time, Luke was unlikely to turn up any more forensic evidence that incriminated her in either case. If he consulted Malc, his mobile would merely inform him that he did not have enough evidence to arrest Constance Robertson for murder. At best, he could charge her with possessing a forged identity card.

"When you went back to London, did you see anyone in or near the house? Apart from Rowan, that is."

"I didn't see Rowan. I told you. And, no, I didn't see anyone."

"Not a thirteen-year-old boy?"

"No."

Luke decided on another bluff. "Well, he saw you. Until next Sunday, I've got a witness, way out of your reach in Cambridge Prison. You can't fiddle with *his* electric supply or take a knife to him. Of course, if he identifies you, the decision to put him to death will be overturned and I'll be back for you. Right now, I'm confiscating your identity card and sending some guards to escort you to Glasgow on a charge of possessing a forged card."

The quickest way of getting Luke from Ballachulish to Cambridge on Monday morning involved a flight from Glasgow to Birmingham. Before Luke boarded the aeroplane at Glasgow Airport, he updated Farrah Bruce on his investigation into her partner's death. He found it impossible to offer her any hope that he would be able to charge Constance Robertson with Lee's murder unless she confessed. Too much time had passed and any traces of a crime would have long since gone. Luke hinted that Farrah would probably have to settle for seeing Lee's killer charged with a different murder, if he could fit the final few pieces together.

In the departure lounge, Malc said to Luke, "I have just been informed that The Authorities regard the charge against Constance Robertson as not sufficiently serious to warrant escorting her to Glasgow and placing her in a holding cell."

"What?" Luke exclaimed. "I don't care about forgery. It's just a way of keeping her locked up till I close Rowan Pearce's murder case – if I can."

"The Authorities can act only on the existing charge against her. At this time, she is not regarded as a murder suspect because someone else has been found guilty. Lee McArthur's death was an accident. There is no overriding reason to reverse these verdicts."

A detached voice announced that the flight to

Birmingham was now boarding.

Getting to his feet and making for the gate, Luke muttered, "The Authorities are fools sometimes."

"By nature, all humans act foolishly occasionally. You have taken the appropriate action to control Constance Robertson's movements. You have taken away the identity card, stopping travel from Ballachulish."

"She managed to move around without a card before."

"The subject's status will be broadcast to telescreens in the area so she will not be able to persuade others to help. In effect, she is under curfew. She is also obliged to report by telescreen to the Glasgow Authorities once every twenty-four hours."

"Mmm. Let's hope it works. She's devious. She's proved that."

Luke stepped into the body of the aeroplane and found his seat. To preserve battery life, Malc settled awkwardly onto the two adjacent seats. Luke looked down at him and, trying to drag himself out of a glum mood, said, "Don't forget to fasten your seatbelt."

"I do not need a seatbelt and it is not designed for my geometry," Malc replied.

"In other words, you don't fit," Luke remarked. "Like Everton Kohter."

"Explain the comparison."

"He's innocent, Malc. He's going to be strapped to a death-cell chair where he doesn't belong. He doesn't fit."

He shook his head sadly. "It should be Camilla. Her scarred fingerprint was near the knife. She had the opportunity and the motive. She's nasty and she had to have the last word. That's what her neighbour said. She went back to kill Rowan because she's vindictive. And she wanted to make sure he'd never poison her new life, the same way she made sure Lee McArthur would never identify her. She couldn't stand the thought of either of them catching up with her."

"Speculation. In law, your beliefs do not substitute for facts."

On the runway, the engines screamed and the aeroplane lurched forwards.

This time when the cab dropped Luke outside Block J, the grim building, its intimidating walkway and security measures were less of a shock. Once inside, Greg Roper marched him through the same bleak passageways to the same interview room. There, Everton Kohter sat with the same empty expression, the same empty eyes. This time, he looked even more gaunt.

Luke gazed at him for a few moments and then said, "I won't waste your time…"

Everton shrugged. He was past caring. His shaven head drooped.

Again, Luke noticed the purple mark of an old wound above his right ear. "I just want you to look at this woman. It's important." Luke pointed at the blank wall opposite

Everton and obediently Malc projected a close-up of Camilla Bunker onto the light green surface. "Have you ever seen her before?"

Everton shrugged again.

"Have a good look before you decide."

The prisoner sighed and peered at the picture. "No." Uninterested, he dropped his eyes. But then something made him look up again.

At once, Luke prompted a response. "Yes? Have you seen her anywhere?"

Everton stared at Camilla's image with a puzzled expression for several seconds. Then, strangely, his face brightened. "Yes! I remember!"

Luke leaned towards him. "What do you remember?"

"I heard a terrible scream. Think so. Wasn't sure with the rain and all. I went towards the house and she came out. Yes. She was the one. She came out. Almost barged into me. In a hurry, she was. Running. I watched her go, I think. I made for the door – she'd left it open – when... I'm not sure. Something happened. But..." Everton lapsed into his own dreamlike state. "It wasn't me! It really wasn't. It was her!"

Everton's mind was clearly in turmoil but, in a bizarre way, he was thrilled.

"I believe you," Luke told him. "But what you said doesn't prove she did it. She admits she was there, not that she killed him. You've got to give me more if I'm going to prove you're innocent. Was Rowan – the man inside – still alive when you went in?"

Shaking his head, Everton muttered, "I don't know. I can't... this is so weird. But it wasn't me!" he repeated gleefully, withdrawing into a world of his own.

Right now, Everton didn't seem to care about proof. Luke guessed that he just wanted to feel freedom from guilt. He relished certainty after two years of not knowing. But Luke's mood was sinking fast. Without undeniable facts, The Authorities and the law would execute someone who now knew he'd done nothing wrong. That was crueller than executing someone who didn't know whether he was guilty or innocent.

Luke wanted to give Everton more than freedom from guilt. Luke wanted to give him complete freedom.

Without emotion, Malc said to Luke, "The prisoner is now behaving conventionally. Blaming someone else is typical behaviour of the guilty."

"And typical of the innocent," Luke snapped at his mobile. He reached across the table and touched Everton's scrawny shoulder. "Can you remember? When she came out, was she stained with anything?"

Everton gave him an empty smile. "Don't know."

In desperation, Luke shook his shoulder. "Think! There must be something else."

But it was hopeless. Everton had retreated again. After all, his own world had to be better for him than the real one.

Chapter Twenty-One

"Doubt is not enough in this case," Malc told Luke. "The evidence against the prisoner is considerable and conclusive. To halt the execution of Everton Kohter, you would have to explain how that amount of forensic data could be wrong and provide new facts that prove his innocence."

"In four days." Annoyed with himself, Luke shook his head. "I'm missing something. I know I am. There's *got* to be something definite that'll clinch it."

It was Wednesday morning and he was walking through Sheffield's Southern Park, hoping that fresh air and relaxation would clear his head. He wanted to forget for a while all of the obvious leads. He wanted to clear away the clutter to reveal some neglected pathway that he could explore for the first time.

He was sure that the answer lay in working out what had happened to Everton that day two years ago when he reached Rowan and Camilla's open front door. It was something that had made him act bizarrely when the FI arrested him and, even today, it prevented his brain from retrieving the memory. Luke couldn't believe that Everton had merely been upset at the sight of Rowan's dead body. Whatever had affected him went well beyond normal shock. It was the key to understanding why he'd made himself appear so guilty.

To Luke's left, there was a long line of evergreens. In the middle, one tree had not thrived as much as its neighbours. It was much shorter than the others and its foliage had turned brown and brittle. Above ground, the height of the adjacent trees deprived it of sunlight and their width deprived it of space. Below ground, its roots could not compete with the bullies on either side. The tree was still standing, but it was dead. Luke gazed at the pathetic thing and thought of Everton.

"What if I got a confession out of Camilla Bunker?"

"That would be regarded as fresh evidence. The death penalty would be delayed, giving you more time to account for the misleading forensic data and establish the reliability of the confession."

"The instructors at school said being an FI wasn't easy. They weren't kidding." Luke came to a standstill again. "I just can't bear the thought of Everton being murdered by The Authorities. That's what it is, when he's innocent. And he's only fifteen!"

"His age is irrelevant."

"Yeah, I know. But…" Luke brushed snowflakes out of his long black hair. "Kill a fifteen-year-old and you've taken sixty-odd years, children, a career, everything. You don't want to get it wrong." Sighing, he flicked the melted snow from his hand and then looked up at the clouds. "It's getting darker. I think we're in for a big snowstorm."

"The weather forecast for Sheffield includes a sixty-five per cent chance of snow."

Already, the flakes were larger and falling more thickly, Luke thought. "Ninety-five per cent is more like it," he murmured.

"I have just received a transmission from the Glasgow Authorities. Constance Robertson did not make contact yesterday. Neighbours report that they have not seen her since she went yachting in the afternoon. There is a team of agents in the area, searching for the subject."

"What?" Luke cried, dismayed by the news.

"I have just received a transmission…"

"No, I heard." Luke took a deep breath. "Make an urgent request for a helicopter, Malc. The Authorities must let me have one this time. I need to be in Ballachulish. Now."

"Transmitting."

"Come on," he said, sprinting for the exit. "I'm going to the helipad. I need to take off before this storm hits."

"I have not yet…"

"And I haven't got the time to hang around, waiting for the go-ahead."

As he dashed back past the stunted and sadly wilting tree, Luke had the overwhelming feeling that it was trying to tell him something.

Luke's headphones reduced the racket from the rotors and engine to a muted drone, similar to the unsettling sound in Jade's latest composition. He could hear the pilot's voice seeking permission to take off and requesting the latest information from the Meteorological Office.

"You have a tight window before the storm will ground you, Five Nine."

With her hands hovering over the joystick and lever, the pilot said, "Repeat that, Control. Are you telling me to abandon the flight?"

"Negative, Five Nine. You have clearance for the next few minutes. Once north of Leeds, you have cold clear outlook."

"Copy, Control. I'm out of here." Straightaway, she operated the lever.

With a jerk, the blades plucked the helicopter from the tarmac. For a moment, Luke felt his stomach lurch uncomfortably. The pilot swivelled the craft so its nose was pointing in the right direction, and then she pushed the joystick forwards. The helicopter pitched and headed north at speed.

At first, she seemed to be flying blind. Wipers swept rapidly to and fro across the window but, beyond them, there was an almost complete whiteout. "Don't worry," her voice said into Luke's ear. "The computer can see even if I can't and we'll be free of it soon. I just hope this mission of yours is important enough."

There was a tiny microphone bent around his cheek and positioned right in front of his mouth. Speaking loudly, he replied, "Yes, I think so."

"Whoa," the pilot said, glancing sideways at him with a smile. "No need to shout. These microphones are pretty good."

"Sorry."

Outside, they flew through a persistent white curtain.

The helicopter's landing skids touched down on an area of flat land outside Ballachulish ferry terminal and the craft settled itself down. Luke thanked the pilot and leapt onto frozen ground. During the flight, they had left the snowstorm behind. The northern sky was clear and a southerly wind was gusting.

At the edge of Lake Leven, Luke was met by one of The Authorities' agents who shouted above the noise of the helicopter, "I think we've cracked it!"

"What's happened?"

The air shuddered with the still rotating blades and Luke had to grasp his hair with both hands to stop it flying across his face in the swirling draught.

The agent led Luke away from the din and yelled, "We've found her yacht. Wrecked."

"Where? Was she in it?"

The agent pointed westwards. "I'll take you. It's ten minutes on foot. A walker spotted something poking out of the water. Turned out to be the tip of the mast. We brought in a lifting barge. The yacht's got a big dent in its bow. Locals say it looks like ice damage."

"She hit an iceberg and more-or-less sank?" Luke queried, pulling up his collar against the wind.

"Uh-huh. Seems so anyway."

"What about her? Have you found her?"

The agent shook his head. "No sign yet."

Luke nodded. "I'm not surprised."

"Why's that?"

"Because she's at it again," Luke answered as he strode along the lakeside walkway. "She's staged another disappearance. Last time it was a plane. This time, a boat. She rammed a big chunk of ice on purpose, went overboard, and swam for the shore, making everyone think she's drowned. All because she knew I was on to her. She thought I was about to produce a witness who'd identify her as a murderer." Even the terrain reminded Luke of the aeroplane crash site. At the edge of the lake, there were trees that would provide good cover for anyone wishing to sneak away. He turned to Malc who, as always, was floating not far from his shoulder. "How long would someone of her build last in water this cold, Malc?"

"It depends on a number of factors such as clothing. Fatal hypothermia from immersion is likely to occur in two to three minutes."

Luke glanced at the agent. "Could a good swimmer get back onto dry land in a couple of minutes from where the boat went down?"

"I should think so. They'd have to scramble over the ice at the edge. You'll see for yourself soon. Won't be long."

"Well, call your team off. I don't want them trampling all over the nearest bit of land. If I'm right, I might be able to pick up her shoeprints in the snow."

"You'd better hurry. The forecast says there's fresh snowfall coming up from the Midlands."

"Yeah," Luke replied. "It was behind me in the helicopter."

A tug, equipped with a crane, had lifted Constance Robertson's tiny yacht out of the lake and balanced it on a hotel's private pier where it lay like a stranded fish. The prow was buckled beyond repair.

"Go over and scan it, Malc," Luke ordered. "The water's probably got rid of any significant traces but go and make sure."

The agent pointed out into the lake. "See that buoy? That marks the spot. It's fairly shallow there. That's why it didn't sink completely."

Luke smiled wryly. "She wouldn't have wanted it to sink without trace. She'd rely on it being spotted."

"What else do you want us to do?"

"I guess I've got to follow procedures, though it won't do any good. Malc's scan can penetrate water to a depth of about a metre but it's deeper than that, isn't it?" Seeing the agent nod, Luke continued, "All right. Dredge as much of this section of the lake as you can before the weather hits us. Just in case. But she'll have gone."

The agent looked pleased with himself and pointed to two boats chugging along in parallel with a net stretched between them. "Uh-huh. Won't be long. Nearly done."

Luke watched them in silence until Malc returned to his side. "Find anything?" he asked.

"I have logged a large number of artefacts. However, most originate from the water or the silt of the lake. I have not detected anything specific to the subject."

"Okay. Search the coast for a hundred metres either side of this position, from the water's edge to the second line of trees. I'm looking for her footprints in the snow. You know her shoe size."

Malc glided away, starting his scan at the furthest point on the western side.

Luke let out a steamy breath. Just a few hours ago, he'd been standing in a Sheffield park, wondering why he was drawn to a dead evergreen, and now he was standing beside an icy lake at Ballachulish, waiting for his mobile to seek out significant footprints on the bank and for some agents to fail to find a woman's body in the water.

But he was wrong.

There was a shout from one of the boats. "We've got something here!"

The agent glanced at Luke and then yelled, "Okay. Bring it to the hotel pier."

Even from where Luke stood, he could see three men leaning over the rail and pulling in the net with their hands.

He watched them push aside a chunk of ice and then heave until a woman's lifeless legs emerged from the water.

He swallowed and his muscles tensed. And he cursed under his breath. The last thing he wanted was Constance Robertson's death. Forcing a confession from her was his best chance of saving Everton Kohter.

At a distance, he couldn't make out the details of the woman's body while the three agents manhandled it onto the deck, but it was clothed and bloated. A rope tied around her waist was attached to a large rock. Luke jogged towards the jetty to meet the boat. Impatiently, he waited for it to dock and then jumped down onto the deck where the men had left their gruesome find.

When Luke saw the woman's face, he came to an immediate standstill and gasped.

Her cheeks had taken on the pink-brown tinge typical of hypothermia. Her tissues would have been too cold to take up oxygen from the blood so they'd become bright pink. No doubt, a post-mortem would find acute ulcers in the stomach lining, sludging of blood in small vessels, and frostbite in her extremities. If she had swallowed cold water, it could have triggered a nervous reflex that would have caused cardiac arrest.

In time, a pathologist's examination would distinguish hypothermia from drowning but, for now, Luke had to figure out why Farrah Bruce had just been scooped out of Lake Leven.

Chapter Twenty-Two

"Malc," Luke shouted at the top of his voice. "Over here. Quickly!"

Seconds later, Luke's mobile was hovering over the unexpected finding, comparing the woman's physical features with his database of people involved in the case. "The victim is not Constance Robertson, also known as Camilla Bunker. It is Farrah Bruce from Glasgow," Malc pronounced. "I suggest you examine her right hand."

Luke knelt down. He took off his woollen gloves and put on medical ones instead because they didn't leave any residue. Then he pulled Farrah's sodden right arm away from her body and laid out her hand on the open deck. Malc was right. There was something in her clenched fist. Grimacing at the unpleasant task, Luke forced up her frozen fingers one-by-one until he revealed a sapphire brooch in the form of a butterfly with a small patch of material attached to it. Luke recognized it at once. It was the brooch that Constance Robertson had worn on her coat. The ripped material told Luke that Farrah must have torn it away in some sort of struggle.

Feeling sick, Luke stood up and took some deep breaths. "You know what's happened here, don't you?" he said. "In a way, it's my fault. I told Farrah all about Constance Robertson because I promised to keep her up-to-date. I didn't realize how bitter she was about Lee. When I said I wouldn't be able to charge Robertson with Lee's murder, I bet she came up here to get her own revenge." Feeling wretched, Luke shook his head. "It backfired. Robertson got the better of her and… this is the result. She weighted the body down, probably hoping it wouldn't be discovered till it was unrecognisable and we thought it was her."

"Unproven speculation."

"Yes, but the brooch is good evidence."

"Confirmed. Finding the prime suspect with a torn coat, or at least matching the fibres, would settle the case, irrespective of the circumstances and motive."

Luke thought about it for a moment and then crouched down again. He felt around Farrah's neck and then searched every one of her pockets. As he expected, he failed to find her identity card. He looked at Malc and said, "Camilla will have taken Farrah's card. If she'd left it on the body, we wouldn't have been fooled into thinking it was Camilla Bunker, no matter how long she'd been under water. And I bet Camilla's pretending to be Farrah Bruce. Put out a general call, Malc. I want to know straight away if anyone anywhere uses Farrah Bruce's identity card."

"Transmitting."

Luke stood upright again. "We've got to find her before she switches to another identity — if she knows another forger – and disappears again. She might've done some research in case she had to do another runner."

"You should alert Sadie Kershaw."

"Good point. I suppose Lee might've mentioned her. Send her a message, Malc. If she gets a visit from someone called Farrah Bruce – or either of her other names – tell her to be very careful, and contact me as soon as she can. Tell her to agree to make a new card and fix up a meeting to hand it over twenty-four hours later. That way, I can be there – with guards."

"Processing."

Luke asked, "Did you find any shoeprints fitting Camilla's size?"

"Confirmed."

"Confirmed? Don't just stand there, then. Take me to them." He looked up at the sky and added, "I've got to track them before they get covered by fresh snow." On the point of leaving, he said to the agent, "Sorry. I can't hang around. Bag up the brooch and bit of material. Then get a pathologist in. Standard procedure for a suspicious death."

"I'm onto it."

The shoeprints led directly away from the lake, through an uphill channel between the trees. Within a few metres, before the rise became very steep, Luke and Malc came across a corridor for electric cabs.

Luke asked, "Where does this go?"

"To the left, it leads back to Ballachulish and the Pass of Glencoe – which is still open. The other direction is considered a picturesque route to the coastal city of Oban. It is lengthy because it has to go round several lakes and mountains. It is used only for leisure. From Oban, many ferry routes are accessible. It is also possible to use the route to travel on to Glasgow."

"Is it passable at the moment?"

"I am trying to establish remote access to transport files."

"Good." Luke did not encroach on the track. He didn't want to spoil the trail of prints. "Which way did she walk? Along the track to call a cab at the nearest card reader, or straight across and up the hill?" It looked to be a daunting climb.

Malc floated forwards, scanning the ground. "She turned right along the track."

"Towards Oban and Glasgow." Luke followed Malc.

"I have located the relevant transport information. The corridor has been cleared of snow. It is passable to Oban and beyond."

The trail stopped abruptly five kilometres down the track at a tiny hamlet called Kentallen where a short string of houses nestled at the base of the mountain. Opposite the homes, there was a transport reader beside the corridor. There, Malc came to a halt.

Immediately, Luke cried, "Of course! She's got nowhere to live. Except she's Farrah Bruce now. She'd sneak into Farrah's quarters in Glasgow. Malc, send guards round to Farrah Bruce's apartment right now."

"Transmitting as a high-priority message."

Luke swiped his card through the reader and said into the microphone, "Urgent travel to Ballachulish." Turning to Malc, he added, "I haven't heard the helicopter take off yet. That's the quickest way to Glasgow. Tell the pilot to wait for me."

The helicopter would have to fly directly towards the coming snowstorm. "I've done the calculations," the pilot said to him through the headphones, "and we're not going to reach Glasgow. The weather's going to force us down before that. I can't afford to be going over mountains when that happens. You really don't want to be stranded up on top. I've plotted a straight course over Glencoe, then I'll follow valleys till the storm hits us. That way, I can land somewhere safe and low down when I have to."

Luke didn't really get a second chance to see the fantastic bird's-eye view of the highland peaks. Cloud and nightfall loomed. Besides, his heart wasn't in it. He just wanted to be in Glasgow.

Beyond Glencoe, the helicopter lurched downwards into a gorge and flew along with great walls of rock on either side until the storm appeared ahead of them. It wiped Lake Lomond from their sight. The voice in Luke's ear said, "I'm taking her down. It's too dangerous to go any further. I can put you next to the corridor."

Luke nodded.

As she manoeuvred the craft on to flat land, the spinning rotors whipped up their own local snowstorm. Luke jumped out into a blinding white swirl.

With his volume set to maximum, Malc said, "This way to the corridor reader."

Luke dashed after him, desperate not to lose sight of his mobile in the blizzard.

As soon as a cab arrived and its door slid back, Luke leapt inside and brushed the snow from his coat. The door closed, shutting out the storm, and the vehicle moved away. It was not able to get up to cruising speed, though. Daylight had diminished almost to nothing. There was little to see but falling snow.

Malc announced bad news. "Guards have informed me that Farrah Bruce's home is empty, but it has been looted."

Luke was staring out of the window, hypnotized by the cascading snow. "She's always a step or two ahead of me," he muttered. "Get them to check if there's any reference to Sadie Kershaw in the apartment."

"Transmitting."

The world outside the cab had become a hazy shadow of the real thing. Sometimes, Luke made out the faint flickering lamps of a village. Sometimes, the cab's lights picked out the sinister shape of a tree beside the corridor. The ghostly figures made Luke think of the evergreens in Southern Park and the trees that were taking over parts of London. They had something in common. Whilst most of them were growing vigorously, one of the Sheffield evergreens had died and Luke remembered that, outside Rowan Pearce's house, there was a dead birch.

Luke pulled down the screen over the window. "Malc. Can you project images onto this?" He pointed at the light grey material.

"Confirmed."

"Did you store any pictures of Rowan Pearce's house when I talked to his neighbour a couple of weeks ago?"

"Yes."

"Show me."

The image brought it all back to Luke. The trees were in better condition than the buildings, apart from that one dead birch. Its branches were brittle and broken. Its trunk was lifeless and almost split into two as if an enormous axe had sliced it down the middle.

"All right," Luke said. "Now give me the picture of Everton Kohter being arrested two years ago."

On the makeshift screen, a confused and dishevelled Everton was standing under an elm, five metres from the front door. Everywhere was saturated. All of the trees were fine, even the birch. Its main trunk had parted into two but it seemed to be alive. "Zoom in on the birch tree, please. Focus on where the trunk's cracked open."

Malc magnified the image.

"Hold it there," Luke said. "Look. Isn't that fresh wood where it's split?"

"Correct. The light colour of the timber suggests that it has been exposed very recently, before weathering darkens it."

"And two years later, it's dead. Why? What happened to it?"

"Unknown."

"Remember, when Everton went towards the door, it was raining. There was a storm. He said it went dark. The neighbour talked about the noise. What if it was a thunderstorm?"

"Your reasoning is valid but its relevance is unclear."

Luke wasn't unclear. His spine tingled because, for the first time, he thought he knew what had happened. "What if it got struck by lightning? Could that split it in half and kill it?"

Malc was silent for several seconds. "That is a well-founded theory. There are scorch marks on the wood."

Luke nodded and grinned. "If lightning hit the tree, it might have struck Everton as well. And you know what I'm thinking?"

"No."

"I think he's still scorched. That purple mark on his head, just above his ear. It reminds me of something

Farrah said about Lee McArthur's hand. It was burnt purple and black by an electric shock. Obviously that's what electricity does. And lightning's a fancy form of electricity. Maybe it gave Everton a purple burn as well."

Malc agreed. "The mark is consistent with lightning damage, but there is insufficient data to be conclusive. Other injuries could cause such a blemish. For example, a stinger leaves a similar burn on human skin."

"That's because a stinger fires a stream of electrified air – like lightning. But that fades. So," Luke said, "tell me the symptoms of being struck by lightning."

"Loss of memory, long-term pain, mental problems, childlike behaviour, Pseudobulbar Affect, scorched muscle, joint problems, changed personality, epileptic fit, and death."

"Epileptic fit!"

"Confirmed. Several cells in a small area near the surface of the brain fire at the same time in an electrical frenzy, creating a seizure."

"Now we're steaming! He heard a scream and went towards the house. Camilla ran out. Just by the door, he got hit by lightning, staggered in and had a fit. There wasn't any evidence of a fight with Everton under Rowan's fingernails because they didn't fight. Rowan was already dead. It makes sense. People having a fit dribble and might wet themselves. That's why he left saliva and urine behind – on himself and the victim. That's why the saliva was smeared out. It wasn't a deliberate spit. And they gnash their teeth. That's how come he bit the body. All the evidence on the floor says he was rolling around, leaving fibres, hair and sweat all over the place. He grabbed furniture and ornaments and knocked them over. He even grabbed the knife – or at least touched it with his fingers, leaving his prints." Luke barely paused for breath. "Rowan was lying in a pool of blood so, when Everton started thrashing about, he would've got blood on his clothing and skin, as well as bruises from bashing himself on everything. You've got to admit, it explains a lot."

"Correct."

"What else did you say? Loss of memory. That's spot-on. Everton doesn't remember a thing. Mental problems? Sure. Plenty. What's Pseudobulbar Affect?

"Patients with Pseudobulbar Affect often laugh uncontrollably at inappropriate times, such as during memorials. Their behaviour is out of character."

Luke had never heard of the bizarre condition, but he nodded knowingly. "Tell me again what was weird about the questioning of Everton Kohter."

"The prisoner laughed frequently and inappropriately."

Luke clenched his fist and punched the air. "Yes!" Then he took a deep breath. "Malc. You said I'd have to explain how so many clues could be wrong. I reckon I've just done it. I want you to request an immediate review of the death sentence passed on Everton Kohter. I must have enough evidence to make his conviction unreliable."

For several seconds, Malc checked the new data against the requirements of the law. Then he said, "I comply with your request. Transmitting as an essential communication to The Authorities."

"Brilliant!"

A machine did not understand the human need to celebrate. Malc did not allow Luke to savour the moment. Programmed to recognize the importance of an incoming message, Malc said, "No references to Sadie Kershaw have been found in Farrah Bruce's quarters, but someone using her identity card has accessed Lee McArthur's computer in the last twenty-four hours. I have searched my copy of his files. Two different documents relate to Sadie Kershaw. One includes her address. This information would be available to anyone browsing the computer."

At once, Luke put aside his feelings of triumph. Now, he had to worry about Sadie Kershaw because he believed that Camilla would visit her to get a new identity card. And Luke knew what Camilla did to people once she'd finished with them. "All right, Malc. Forget the trip to Glasgow. Plot a route direct to Derby. Maximum possible speed. And get me a sound-only link to Sadie Kershaw."

Chapter Twenty-Three

The mesmerizing stream of white flakes shone in the vehicle's lights. But Luke thought he'd detected a lessening of the blizzard and the cab seemed to have picked up pace. He could only hope that he would soon emerge from the other side of the snowstorm and head for Derby at top speed.

"Sadie Kershaw's home computer is refusing to establish a link," Malc told him.

"What?" Luke cried in astonishment. "Can it do that? Can it refuse an FI?"

"Under normal circumstances, no."

Puzzled, Luke asked, "So, what's not normal about it?"

"I am on-line to her system and she has blocked verbal communication while she works on a high-priority task."

Luke nodded. "I bet that means Sadie can't speak because Camilla's with her. She's working on another identity card."

"Procedure requires you to send in guards if you believe the prime suspect is present," Malc replied.

"Mmm." Luke looked out of the window. The snowfall was definitely less dense. He said to Malc, "Sadie's safe till she finishes making the card. And she knows the situation because you sent her that message. If she's got any sense — and I reckon she's got lots — she'll play for time. Can you place a document in her computer that she can open when no one's looking?"

"Confirmed."

"All right. Tell her I'm on my way. Give her your best estimate of arrival time and tell her to stall if Camilla's with her. Then, I want you to request a team of guards. At least twenty, but not to barge in. Tell them to surround the block where Sadie lives, but not to show themselves. They do nothing till I get there. It's too dangerous. If Camilla gets a whiff of them, she might turn on Sadie."

"Processing tasks. However, you should note that a person in a building would not be able to smell human beings outside it."

"I wish you wouldn't take me so literally." Luke took the edge off his grumble with a smile. Then, aware of a sudden transformation outside, he looked out of the window. The air was clear and a full moon lightened the evening. The cab had come out of the northbound blizzard and accelerated. Ahead, the corridor was thick with fallen snow. "Make sure the route's open all the way to Derby, Malc. I don't have time to wait, so get snowploughs out now if anywhere's blocked by drifts."

The storm had left Derby several centimetres deep in soft snow. Against a lot of the buildings, huge drifts had collected. As Luke made his way down the brightly lit walkway to Sadie's apartment block, the snow

195

cushioned his every step. His boots scrunched the stuff and packed it down into clear impressions of his soles. Closer to her home, more footprints gave away the position of the ring of guards. Luke nodded towards a couple of them as he passed. "Stay in place, please. If anyone comes out of her block, stop them. Okay?"

Sadie's apartment was at the rear of the building so, when he approached the main entrance, Luke knew that no one could look out of her quarters and see him. He swiped his identity card through the reader and the main door sprang back for him. Inside, a cold draft was coming down the passageway towards the elevator because, at the far end, the fire exit had been forced open. Luke imagined that the splintered door was Camilla's work. She would have had to break in because the entrance would not have responded to Farrah Bruce's identity card. It would open only for residents, service engineers and forensic investigators.

He went up to the third floor and tiptoed along the hallway until he reached Sadie's quarters. As an FI, Luke had an identity card that would open her door but he had no idea what to expect on the other side of it. "You are at full power, aren't you?" he whispered to Malc.

"Confirmed. I recharged in the cab."

"Okay. Defence mode. Whatever happens, protect Sadie."

"I cannot comply. My programming allows no

flexibility. I must protect you first."

"All right. But just make sure she doesn't get hurt."

"I should enter first," said Malc.

Luke nodded and held out his identity card towards the security panel beside the door. "Ready?"

"Confirmed."

Luke pushed his card against reader. The door slid back and at once Malc flew into the living quarters. Luke followed, but came to an immediate halt. Beyond the open glass panel that extended from the floor to the ceiling, Camilla was standing at the edge of the balcony. In her right hand, she held a stinger. Her other hand steadied Sadie's unconscious body which was lying untidily and horizontally along the rail.

Through the open window, Camilla smirked at him. "You're becoming a nuisance, you know, Harding. But you can forget the element of surprise. Her computer flashes up a security message, identifying anyone who comes in the main entrance."

Once again, Camilla was a step ahead of him.

Luke did not need Malc to tell him that Sadie was still alive. By the lamps above the balcony, Luke could see little puffs of condensation as she breathed in the chill night air. Luke switched his gaze to the electric plasma gun. "Have you stunned her?"

"What does it look like?"

"It looks like an assault with a stinger. I'm guessing it's

what you did with Farrah on the boat before you pushed her in. The trouble is, she woke up and grabbed your brooch, didn't she?" He pointed at the tear in her coat. "I've got her body and your little blue butterfly."

Camilla grunted angrily. "She was following me. So, I let her. I stunned her down by the pier. The rest was easy. I bundled her on board and weighed her down with a rock. But as soon as I got her into the water, she came round and struggled..." She looked down at the rip. "The cold got her quicker than I thought. She went down with my brooch."

Luke was bristling with tension but tried to look calm and in control. "My mobile can put you out of action any time I tell him to fire."

She laughed. "Why did you think I put Sadie here? If I let go," she said, glancing down at her hostage, "over she goes."

"Okay," Luke replied, knowing that she had trumped him. "But you can't get away and you know I've got enough evidence to charge you with the murder of Farrah Bruce."

"So, it doesn't matter to me if I kill Sadie as well. You can't give me more than one death sentence. Send your mobile away. Then we can talk about my terms for letting her live. A hostage and a stinger put me in charge. I *can* get away. You know it."

Luke could feel cold drops of sweat running down his

back and soaking into his shirt. He shook his head. "Malc's programming won't allow him to leave."

"Overrule it. If you don't, I'll let go and you can watch her fall. We're a long way up."

Staring at Camilla, Luke was convinced that she would take Sadie's life with barely a thought. "Okay." He turned to Malc and said, "I'm giving you a direct order to leave the building."

Searching his set of instructions for guidance, Malc hovered for several seconds without responding.

"Drift out of the window," Luke told him.

"Hang on," Camilla snapped. "Don't try anything silly. It can come out of the window, but nowhere near me."

Luke put up both palms. "No tricks. I haven't told him to do anything apart from get out. You heard it all."

"Okay," she muttered. "That way." With the stinger, she gestured towards the furthest point of the balcony.

"Fair enough," Luke replied. He was relying on the fact that his mobile would take his order literally. Once Malc had glided through the window, he had fulfilled the instruction to leave the building. Luke trusted that Malc would stay within recording distance but remain hidden somewhere outside. Luke also hoped that his mobile had interpreted his second instruction correctly. Trying to make certain, he added, "Drift below the balcony."

The place was eerily quiet apart from Malc's hushed whirring. Eventually, he replied. "I will comply."

Camilla's eyes followed the mobile suspiciously as he made his way deliberately through the window, across the balcony and plunged downwards, out of sight. Then she stared angrily at Luke. "Right. We're equals now. I can see you want to play the hero and get this sad specimen back alive. To do that, you're going to have to do some things for me."

"Like what?"

"Guarantee me safe passage to a cab and an overseas plane."

"You want me to let you off three counts of murder! That's what you're saying." He ran his fingers nervously through his thick crop of hair.

"Yes. Exactly."

Luke showed no outward sign of triumph, but he had just tempted Camilla into admitting that she had killed three times. He trusted that Malc was close enough to record her response. "The Authorities will have something to say about that."

"If you want Sadie back, you don't have a choice. You agree to my demands." To make her point, Camilla shifted the hand that kept Sadie balanced on the rail. Her limp body wobbled dangerously.

Luke racked his brains for the best option, resembling Malc when he was caught in a dilemma not covered by his programming. He had tried to give Malc a coded message but maybe his mobile had not understood because he was not reappearing behind Camilla and Sadie. Perhaps Luke was on his own this time. "I haven't been in this position before," he said. "I could contact The Authorities – if I had my mobile – and see if they agree to a deal."

Camilla laughed. "You're just a little boy lost without your toy! No. It's just you and me. When Sadie's conscious, you clear the way to the freeway and get us a cab. No one's going to question you. You're an FI."

"I'll do it if you leave Sadie here and take me as your hostage."

"No. She's a much better bargaining tool."

Luke was caught in an impossible standoff. He had to agree to Camilla's terms and hope that, at some point, he had an opportunity to pounce. "All right. I'll take you to Birmingham Airport." He took a step towards her.

"Back off!" she shouted, pointing the stinger directly at him with her finger on the trigger. "I don't trust you."

"If you want me to get you to the airport, you won't shoot," he said, hoping that he was right.

"I will if I have to."

In that instant, Luke was distracted. Outside, Malc rose up behind Camilla. A narrow red guide-beam came from him, pinpointing Camilla's right arm, a few centimetres up from the stinger. Without hesitation, before Luke could shout a command, Malc fired his laser. The beam flashed from the mobile to Camilla like a streak of lightning.

Immediately, Camilla cried out in pain and dropped the stinger. Her left hand jerked up and clutched at the purple scorch mark on her right arm.

Without support, Sadie rolled off the balcony railing and fell noiselessly.

Chapter Twenty-Four

Luke reacted first. He darted forwards, through the open window, and picked up the stinger. Training it on Camilla, he shouted to his mobile, "Guards in here now!"

"Transmitting."

Camilla was doubled up, nursing her arm.

"Keep watch on her," Luke said to Malc. He leaned over the balcony and looked down. Sadie had fallen into a deep snowdrift a long way below him. The soft snow had cushioned her weight. Anxiously, he asked, "Is she all right?"

"I detect life signs within normal limits."

"Get a medical team here anyway."

"I calculated that the impact would cause only acceptable damage."

Relieved, Luke managed a weak smile at last. "You got my message, then."

"You use language skilfully. Therefore, when you made the ambiguous statements, 'Drift out of the window', and 'Drift below the balcony,' I assumed you wanted me to act on both interpretations. I left the building via the window and checked if there was a snowdrift underneath the balcony where the hostage would fall."

Camilla looked up and swore at them both.

Luke grinned at her. "It's amazing what a little boy lost

and his toy can do, isn't it?" He turned back to Malc and asked, "Did you pick up the conversation in here?"

"Confirmed. The sound quality is poor because it was recorded at a distance, but it is adequate for the purposes of the law. I have filed it in case notes."

"Including the bit about three murders?"

"Yes. You have sufficient evidence to charge Camilla Bunker with the murders of Rowan Pearce, Lee McArthur and Farrah Bruce."

Three armed guards crashed into the room and the case was at an end. With a huge sense of relief, Luke handed over both Camilla Bunker and the stun gun.

The next morning, after Luke had slaughtered a pomegranate in Sheffield Hotel and refreshed himself with a shower, a middle-aged man appeared on his telescreen. Wearing the badge of a member of The Authorities, he began, "Thank you, FI Harding. Your investigation of the Everton Kohter conviction was very thorough. Your case is going before the relevant committee and I'm sure it will get a sympathetic hearing. Well done. You have saved us a certain amount of embarrassment."

Luke interrupted. "Embarrassment?" he spluttered. "It's a boy's life!"

"Indeed. I hope you have been as conscientious in probing alleged corruption by Sheffield Pairing Committee. I'm eager to hear your findings, but it will have to wait until tomorrow. Today, I'm recalling your mobile aid to law and crime for a major service. A lack of communication regarding the corruption case suggests that it has a fault. This will be diagnosed and rectified today. Your mobile will be returned to you tonight so that you can present your report tomorrow morning."

"But..."

"There can be no objections. This is an immediate emergency recall."

Sadie Kershaw glanced at the time showing on her telescreen. "It's nearly one o'clock in the morning!" she exclaimed. "And the doctor said I've got to rest."

"Yes. Sorry. How are you feeling?" Luke walked into the familiar quarters in Derby with Malc behind him.

"Two broken ribs. Sore, but okay."

Luke nodded sympathetically, but he didn't linger on her injuries. He had something important to do. "I'm up in front of The Authorities tomorrow. Strictly, I mean later today, I suppose. Anyway, pairing and forgery will be on the agenda."

"You've come to warn me."

"Not really," Luke replied. "I've come for your help. Listen to this." He turned towards Malc and said, "Define skeleton in the cupboard."

"A skeleton is the supportive rigid structure or framework of..."

"Stop," Luke commanded. "What about the meaning of the whole phrase?"

"It means that a collections of bones has been found…"

Interrupting, Luke said to Sadie, "You see? A week ago, he knew that skeleton in the cupboard meant hiding a guilty secret because I told him to put it in his memory. But it's gone. Worse, he doesn't know some vital facts about the Chair of the Sheffield Pairing Committee and the behaviour of The Authorities."

Sadie replied, "The poor thing's lost its memory. Like you expected."

"Mmm. If you want some protection in the morning – and you want the truth to come out – you'd better let him download all the missing stuff from the copy on your system."

"Sure. It's at work. My computer here wasn't big enough, but we can do it through an on-line link. It'll take a while with that much data to sift."

Luke checked the time. "It's all right. I've got eight and a half hours."

"Don't you investigators sleep, then?"

"Not with this on my mind."

Chapter Twenty-Five

With Malc at his side, Luke stood in a conference room of Sheffield City Hall. Facing him, behind a large desk, were Nicoletta Boniwell and three unfamiliar members of The Authorities. As Luke delivered his explosive report, they all gazed at him with dour and serious faces. He felt as if he were on trial.

"So," he concluded, "Ms Boniwell's committee is entirely innocent of arranging an inappropriate and unconventional pairing because The Authorities approved it. Mollie Gazzo and Rufus Vile were allowed to become partners only for the sake of setting me up. The fact that they used tobacco illegally made them ideal. It looked like corruption that way." Gazing at Nicoletta, he said, "The Authorities wondered if I'd try to bribe you when I found out. But what would you want with bucketfuls of cigarettes when you don't smoke them?" He would have liked to laugh casually but he was far too stressed. "It's all a pretence, isn't it? Sadie Kershaw's genuine but the rest is make-believe."

He had succeeded in stunning the panel.

The Chair of the meeting looked at his colleagues and they whispered together for a while. Then he said, "Your mobile has just been serviced. Our engineer didn't find any data that supports what you say about The Authorities' role in this investigation."

Trying to stay cool, Luke shrugged. "That's strange, because it *was* all there. I thought it was so important, I kept a copy and reinstalled it last night."

"You did what?" The Chair stared at him for several seconds. Then he switched his gaze to Malc. "Is this true?"

"Confirmed," Malc replied. "I can provide…"

The Chair put up his hand. Turning on Luke, he said, "You are implying that The Authorities are corrupt."

"I've supplied the facts to conclude the case. That's all. My mobile will use them to come to a conclusion about The Authorities and the legal implications."

Malc wasn't tense. He wasn't sweating. He wasn't worrying about his future. He said, "There is sufficient evidence to indicate that The Authorities, acting through Mollie Gazzo, incited Sadie Kershaw to commit the crime of forgery."

Luke did not need to say another word.

The four members huddled together and talked urgently in hushed tones.

"Right," the Chair said with an edgy grin. "You've done very well, FI Harding. There's something you need to know that you weren't told at school when under instruction in criminology. It was deliberately hidden from you, as it's hidden from all newly qualified forensic investigators. Soon after graduating, every FI is put through a test of competence, just to make sure they are acting correctly. You've just passed that test with distinction."

Luke looked puzzled. For a moment, it made sense. The whole corruption case was like a school exercise but conducted for real in the outside world. That's why he'd been set up. He *had* been on trial. But, a split-second later, he realized that The Authorities were probably attempting to get themselves out of a predicament by hastily inventing a fantasy. But he couldn't be sure. He glanced towards Malc as if for help. "Do you know anything about this?"

Malc was concerned only with the truth. "If there were a test of competence, there would be examples of forensic investigators losing their status soon after qualification, or returning to school for extra training. I find no record of either."

Luke gazed at the members of the panel. "Thanks, Malc. That's... very useful."

The Authorities' representatives leaned towards each other again and whispered even more frantically. When they parted, the Chair took a deep breath. "Luke, you – and your mobile – are correct. In our efforts to assess your loyalty, we may have been – how shall I put it? – rather too zealous. You've found us out. It isn't our normal practice to contravene the law for our own convenience. I'd go as far as saying it was a mistake. But it serves no purpose to prosecute The Authorities. That would only undermine people's confidence in us. So," he said, "taking into account your excellent performance so far, we feel you should be offered compensation."

"You're going to offer me something to drop a case of incitement to commit a crime and perverting the course of justice?"

"Put crudely, yes."

This was it. The moment that Luke had been dreading and craving in equal measure. It was time to play his own game. "That's fine," he said in a trembling voice, "as long as compensation involves wiping Sadie Kershaw's slate clean. If she got charged with forgery, the facts Malc would provide at her trial would be very awkward for you, I would've thought." Luke tried to ignore the hammering in his chest and his churning stomach. Fixing his gaze on Nicoletta, he added, "And then there's me and Jade Vernon. I'm sure the Pairing Committee could look again at our situation."

"This *is* beginning to sound like bribery." The Chair exchanged quiet words with Nicoletta and then delivered his verdict. "We agree that Ms Kershaw should not be pursued. That's your compensation. The other matter is much more complicated and difficult. If an investigator were paired with a musician, it would undermine our traditions and our principles. If it became known – and it couldn't be kept secret – the floodgates would open. Our way of life would be threatened. So, we refuse your request. Even so," he said, leaning forwards, "we'll look again into the definition of Jade Vernon's job.

I understand you regard her as an assistant forensic investigator. If there is continuing evidence that — alongside her music — she supports your investigations, there may be some flexibility. We make no promises, but, in time, it may become appropriate to reclassify her as an occasional scientist. If that were the case, her pairing situation might be reconsidered. Your mobile is instructed to record any forensic activity undertaken by Jade Vernon. And that," he said, sitting upright again, "is the end of it. There will be no more demands."

It wasn't the clear-cut result that Luke wanted, but it wasn't complete failure. It was somewhere between the two. And he could tell from the faces of the panellists that, no matter how much he threatened, he would not squeeze another drop out of them. He nodded and forced himself to say, "Thank you." Then he turned and walked away with his faithful mobile at his shoulder.

Chapter Twenty-Six

At dawn on Sunday the twelfth of February, a solemn Greg Roper stood erect by the door. For him, the ritual was all-important. The prisoner was marched towards him between two burly guards. Greg brought the group to a halt by putting up his palm. Then he turned and passed his identity card over the release button and the massive arched door swung slowly open.

Sunlight streamed into the large reception and Everton Kohter squinted. He was not used to cold clear daylight.

"That's it," Mr Roper said. "The world. It's all yours. Here's your identity card. Your conviction has been erased and your medical files updated. In the nicest possible way, I hope I never see you again."

Overwhelmed, Everton said nothing. And he didn't move.

To make sure the former inmate understood, Greg thrust the plastic card at him and said, "You can go. You're free."

Luke Harding and Owen Goode were standing at the other end of the forbidding passageway. As always, Malc hovered behind. They waited and watched as Everton began his walk to freedom between the brick walls topped with razor wire and icicles, leaving behind the bleak building with its turrets and armed guards, and its empty Death Cell.

Owen raised his hand in greeting and shouted, "Everton! Come on. Remember me? Owen."

Scared, Everton came to a halt and glanced over his shoulder. He had not even crossed the drawbridge that lay over the deep moat. By the terrified expression on his face, Luke guessed that he wished he could turn back. But Greg was standing in the doorway, as if to prevent his return.

Everton started to walk unsteadily again. As soon as he reached the strong ironwork barrier, it lifted vertically to let him through. With incredulity on his face, he watched it rise up.

Owen said, "Come on. You're out of there."

Everton staggered forwards. When the gate crashed down behind him, his shoulders began to shake. Disorientated, he burst into tears. Great big drops of salty water ran down his cheeks.

"Hey! Don't be daft," said Owen, grabbing Everton by the arms. "It's champion. You're free."

Everton shook his head, totally unable to cope with the release.

"What's wrong?" Owen asked him.

"I don't know…"

"Take your time," Luke said. "It's going to be tough to adjust, I guess."

"In there," Everton muttered, "every day was the same. I knew exactly what was going to happen." He swallowed and surveyed the unfamiliar terrain like a nervous lost animal. "I don't know what's going to happen to me out here. It's too big. I don't know… anything."

"If it helps," Luke said, "I contacted my old instructors at Birmingham School. I told them all about you. If you want, they'll look after you till you're up to scratch. They'll take you as a student and help you catch up as well. That'd give you a bit of certainty."

"Birmingham? But that's…" Everton's eyes glazed over. Apparently, he regarded the city as a faraway paradise. "I've never…"

"Well, it's up to you. On the outside, *you* choose."

Everton looked at Owen and then shifted his gaze back to Luke. "Will you come and see I'm okay?"

"Sure will," Owen answered.

Luke nodded. "You'll have your own telescreen. I'll use it to check everything's good for you. It's a nice school. I bet you'll like it."

Everton sniffed and wiped the moisture from his cheeks and nose with his hand. "All right. Birmingham."

Owen beamed. "Got to be better than here," he said, jerking his head at Block J of Cambridge Prison. "Even school's better than the Death Cell."

Here is the first chapter of the next brilliant **Traces** *story,* **Final Lap**. *Read on for a taste of more forensic crime-solving with Luke and Malc.*

TRACES: FINAL LAP

Chapter One

Everything was wrong. It was the wrong time of year and the sports stadium was unfinished. The crowd was not really a crowd at all. An assortment of trainers, athletes, reporters and enthusiasts was bunched together in the only stand that had been completed so far. Seen from the airship overhead, they were a small oasis in a concrete desert and the builders crawling busily over the rest of the arena looked like worker ants.

Only one competitor had re-entered the stadium and embarked on the final lap. Approaching the end of the marathon, his gasps left a trail of steam behind him in the cold air. The weather was all wrong as well.

The giant telescreen at the far end of the oval was blank. When the electronics were fully installed, it would show pictures taken by the airship and outside cameras, trackside close-ups, and a list of the exact location of every runner in the marathon. For now, the leader's triumph was unannounced, but the large timer was showing 2:08:13.7.

Jed Lester shook his head in disbelief. Without taking his eyes off the front runner in the sky-blue kit, he said to Owen, "He's good, but the organizers are going to have to check the clock or the route. It's a practice run, out of season, and he's too young, but he's coming in not far short of the national record. They've probably messed up the distance."

Owen Goode nodded. "Likely, it's short of the full forty kilometres."

The construction workers on the opposite stand stopped what they were doing and watched the lone runner completing a circuit of the track.

The event was a strange spectacle, designed to test Hounslow's preparations for hosting the International Youth Games in the spring. The volunteer runners were putting the planned marathon route through its paces. The organizers were also checking the electronic timing system, the orientation of the airship, and a tagging device that monitored the position and order of every competitor throughout the long-distance event. After the finish, they would also test the newly completed laboratory for detecting and measuring performance-enhancing drugs.

Jed had been a middle-distance runner. Twenty years ago, he was the best over fifteen hundred metres. Now, he'd teamed up with fifteen-year-old Owen Goode to develop a sports club in Greenwich. They were converting the old domed warehouse, built in a loop of the Thames, into an indoor track and training facility. Already, it was becoming a popular haunt for rebellious London kids who had run away from their schools. Jed was hoping to spot a new generation of athletes among them. He'd entered one boy and two girls into the trial marathon. Right now, he expected them to be twelve to eighteen minutes away from the stadium.

Perplexed by the leader's performance, Jed stroked his trademark bald head with a cold hand and glanced down at the list he'd been given. "Ford Drayton. On this showing, he'll be selected for the Games if the distance and time are right. But something's got to be wrong."

From across the other side of the track, there was a loud clunk and a metallic squeal. Thunderous hammering, pounding, shouting and drilling had become commonplace during the construction of the stadium, so no one took any notice. The noises were followed by a fearsome mechanical groan. Two builders, standing way up high on scaffolding, were resting their elbows on the steel rail and looking down at the closing stages of the race. From their lofty position, they could probably also see the other runners labouring along the outside walkway towards the stadium. Almost certainly, they'd be able to appreciate the full extent of Ford Drayton's lead over the following pack.

Watching Ford's unflagging finish, Owen commented,

"Maybe he's had a bit of help from drugs."

"I don't think so. It's not like it's a power event." Jed stared at Ford's wiry body as he came past the spectators' stand. "It's not his technique that's wrong, for sure," Jed said in admiration. "Look at his posture, how he holds his head. His arms pump beautiful and his coordination's near perfect, even after that distance. But if you're right and he has taken something, he'll be disgraced in an hour or two. That's Lapped for you." Thinking of the Laboratory Analytical Procedure for Performance-Enhancing Drugs, Jed grunted. "In my day, lapped was something that happened to you on the track if you weren't much good. Back then, I had to race – and beat – the cheats. Simple as that."

Before Ford Drayton reached the finishing line, there was an alarming creak from one section of the scaffolding. The sound was followed by a dreadful twang as the bolts holding up the platform on the left-hand side gave way. The planks of wood tilted and then tumbled down towards the running track. The two builders who had been standing on them were tipped sideways as the boards slid out from under their feet. In panic, they both grabbed the bar they'd been leaning against. But the rail also came adrift from the rest of the contraption and the men were pitched into empty air.

Every face in the stand looked up – away from Ford's victory. Steel poles, three planks of wood, a girder, and two men plummeted to the ground. Yet their plunge seemed to last a lifetime. Their arms wheeled and legs flailed in slow motion.

A protracted human scream tore the atmosphere. It was followed by the thud of wood hitting the trackside area and the clatter of a girder and steel railings. One of the metal shafts stabbed into the earth like an oversized javelin. But worst was the silence that followed the dull thumps of the builders hitting the ground.

Focusing on his performance, maintaining his style in spite of exhaustion, Ford Drayton kept an eye on the stadium clock and paid no attention to the commotion behind him. He ran to the finish in stunned silence. Only one spectator – his own trainer – applauded his remarkable achievement.

Forensic Investigator Luke Harding was listening carefully as the face on his telescreen described his next assignment. She was telling him about two construction workers who'd lost their lives in the main sports stadium at Hounslow in the London area. Luke was puzzled, though. He asked, "Do you know for sure it's suspicious? A scaffolding collapse sounds like an accident to me. Or shoddy work."

The representative of The Authorities seemed put out that Luke was questioning her word. She was probably aware that FI Harding had a growing reputation for dissent. Despite his youth, though, he also had a growing reputation for solving difficult cases. "It might sound like an accident to you, taken in isolation. But this isn't the first mishap at the Hounslow development. It began two years ago with an air traffic accident. I believe you know about it."

"Oh, yes," Luke replied. "I came across it in my last case. A Hounslow-to-Glasgow flight. Its fuel line was iffy. Someone in maintenance fitted the wrong nut. The pipe loosened in flight and fuel poured out."

"That's right. And one of the indoor sports venues went up in flames some months ago. It had to be rebuilt. The first manager has gone missing and there have been other incidents as well. I'll download details into your mobile aid to law and crime. We accept that accidents happen. But not this many. There comes a point when bad luck begins to look deliberate. We've reached that point. So, you'll investigate possible sabotage at the site."

"Have there been any deaths apart from the passengers in the plane and these two builders?" he asked.

"Aren't they enough?" she responded. "We want you to catch the person or persons responsible before anyone else dies, and we want to know what happened to Libby Byrne. She was the site manager until she vanished. Her disappearance may or may not have anything to do with her work." The voice of The Authorities paused before adding, "There's a lot at stake here, Investigator Harding.

Hounslow's a high-profile regeneration project. The biggest in the south of England by some distance. Despite the... difficulties, we're on the final lap as far as construction's concerned. We don't want the International Youth Games jeopardized at this late stage. If it fails, it'll be our last attempt to renovate an area of London."

"That'd be a pity." Luke was wondering if she was threatening to axe Owen Goode's alternative school in Greenwich as well.

"Make sure it doesn't happen, then."

"I'll do my best," Luke said towards her fading face.

When the Principal of the Sheffield Music Collective appeared at Jade Vernon's door, she pulled her headphones down from her ears and let them rest on her shoulders, making a strange outsize necklace. She clicked the *Save* button to keep the samples she'd added to a new mix of one of her pieces, and swivelled towards him.

"Sorry to interrupt," he said, "but I've got some news you'll want to hear."

"Oh?"

"Good news," he stressed, beaming like a child. "It's from The Authorities and I think you'll be pleased. Very pleased."

At once, Jade's thoughts turned to pairing. She was sixteen – four years from The Time – and she was hoping that The Authorities might have had a change of heart. Perhaps they would couple her with Luke Harding when The Time came. But would the Head of the Collective get involved in the business of the Sheffield Pairing Committee? Would he even know about her pairing situation and her wishes?

"Oh?" she repeated, wondering how long he was going to keep her in suspense.

"It's an honour for you and the whole Collective," he said. "The Authorities have commissioned you to compose the music for the opening ceremony of the International Youth Games and the official anthem." He'd clearly got more to say but he hesitated to let the glitzy task sink in and to watch her reaction.

Her frown turned into a wide grin. "Really? The anthem? That's... brilliant. Amazing." In her excitement, she jumped to her feet and the headphone cable nearly throttled her. "Fantastic. Why me, though?"

The principal replied, "Don't be so modest, Jade. It's obvious. You were selected because you're good. The best person for the job. Given the occasion, it's also appropriate for a youth – someone less than twenty – to provide the music."

Jade shook both of her fists in the air. "Yes! Fame at last."

"True. Previous writers of sports anthems have gone on to great things. I wish you well with it – as does everyone in the Collective."

"I can hardly believe it, but... I'll need a site visit," Jade said. "To get a feel for the place, to see what would work. Is that all right?"

"I assumed you'd ask so I've already checked. The main stadium is nearly complete so you can visit by arrangement almost any time. The other venues are at various stages of construction. Someone will take you wherever you want to go as long as it's safe and doesn't interfere with the building."

"It's down near London, isn't it?" She tried not to pull a face.

The Principal laughed. "Don't let that put you off. Think of yourself as part of the Hounslow regeneration scheme. It's a golden opportunity."

Despite the need to go to the south, she tingled all over. "I can't wait to get going," she said.

ix